Marcello Fois

THE
ADVOCATE

Translated from the Italian by
Patrick Creagh

THE HARVILL PRESS
LONDON

First published with the title *Sempre Caro*, by Edizioni Frassinelli, Milan, 1998
2 4 6 8 10 9 7 5 3 1
Copyright © Edizioni Frassinelli, 1998
English translation copyright © Patrick Creagh, 2001

Marcello Fois has asserted his right under the Copyright, Designs
and Patents Act 1988 to be identified as the author of this work

First published in Great Britain in 2003 by
The Harvill Press
Random House, 20 Vauxhall Bridge Road,
London SW1V 2SA

Random House Australia (Pty) Limited
20 Alfred Street, Milsons Point, Sydney,
New South Wales 2061, Australia

Random House New Zealand Limited
18 Poland Road, Glenfield,
Auckland 10, New Zealand

Random House South Africa (Pty) Limited
Endulini, 5A Jubilee Road, Parktown 2193, South Africa

The Random House Group Limited Reg. No. 954009
www.randomhouse.co.uk/harvill

A CIP catalogue record for this book
is available from the British Library

ISBN 1 86046 904 3

Papers used by Random House are natural,
recyclable products made from wood grown in sustainable forests;
the manufacturing processes conform to the environmental
regulations of the country of origin

Designed and typeset in Bembo by Libanus Press, Marlborough, Wiltshire

Printed and bound in Great Britain
by Biddles Ltd, Guildford & Kings Lynn

To Francesco Olla

I

THIS IS THE WAY MY FATHER TOLD ME THE STORY. It seems that Bustianu was off on his own, taking his after-lunch stalk up the hill to stretch his legs. What he called his "ever belovèd".

Yes, this was the name he gave to that daily trek, as in Leopardi's poem, *L'infinito*: "Ever belovèd was this secluded hill". To be exact, when Bustianu said "ever belovèd" he didn't mean the hill itself, he meant going to enjoy the cool up there on the mountain, and gazing out at the view and the grazing flocks and getting a breath of fresh air, because in our parts when it's hot it's hot and no two ways about it.

My father told me that people said the man seemed lost in thought, as always when he had a difficult case to deal with. One thing you couldn't accuse him of was not taking his work seriously. In the Court of Assizes he was tireless, and anyone who entrusted their case to him knew that all that could possibly be done would indeed be done. But not for the money! Perish the thought! My father once said he told him: "*Chie tenet dinare comparit innozente, s'abbocà!*" – if you have the money, Avvocato, you'll always get off. And he tells me that Bustianu looked him straight in the eye with one of those typical smiles of his, and shrugged his shoulders. "*Zommari*", said he (for my father's name was Giovanni Maria), "*su dinare non fachet lezze!*" Money, in short, is not what determines the Law.

Actually he pretty often defended for nothing, but all the same he had his reward, earning the respect of the whole community. Fact is, he wasn't on the bread-line. There were some worse off than he was, as it is with everyone, and we're not claiming to say anything original.

So he was lost in thought, his case wasn't going well and his defendant had taken to the hills.

He was defending a youngster, a relative of the Portapanni clan who lived at the Contone, and his mother, Tzia Rosina, made bread and pastries which she sold right there in the house. Such superfine pastries they were that she didn't have time to meet all the orders. People came to her from as far away even as Orgòsolo. And that's saying something, in those days!

Anyway, this woman's son, Zenobi, a fair-haired, blue-eyed wonder of young manhood, had got into trouble at the very end of December over a question of certain head of livestock that had disappeared, and it was made out that he had something to do with it. In short, right out of the blue he was accused of stealing some lambs to sell off and pocket the proceeds.

So his mother, in due time, goes to see Bustianu, all got up in her embroidered headscarf and lace-trimmed apron:

"*S'abbocà*, this is none of my son's doing, and I know him inside out! You must defend him, because to you they'll listen, you're an important person, tell me how much it'll cost, that's all."

"He must give himself up. If he remains a fugitive from justice the whole thing becomes more difficult."

"He won't hear of it, do you think I haven't told him so myself? I've told him it would be better to put himself in the hands of the Law, because he hasn't done anything wicked. But you know as well as I do, if you don't have friends at court . . . "

"And what did he say?"

"Nothing, that he had nothing to do with it, that they've played a dirty trick on him. If you were to see him, *s'abbocà*, you wouldn't recognize him, all skin and bones, and covered in filth . . . Ah, my son!"

"No, no, none of that! Sit down and dry your eyes. What did you tell the Carabinieri when they came to fetch him?"

"That he wasn't at home. What was I supposed to say?"

"Didn't you tell them that your son had been away from Nùoro for two days?"

"Ah yes, that too."

"Away from Nùoro where, exactly?"

"Away from Nùoro, how can anyone know these things for certain? Thanks be to God, Zenobi is of age. It's not as if I had him still at the breast, *s'abbocà*".

"All right, never mind. But if I'm going to defend him we can take that for granted. Now take a minute or two to think, make yourself comfortable and then tell me everything, down to the last detail."

* * *

There she was sitting in front of me. A tiny little person. All got up in her Sunday best. She told me that that late December evening when Sergeant Arturo Poli, temporarily in command of the local Carabinieri station, his superior having been transferred elsewhere, presented himself at the door of her cottage, her whole life came to a complete stop. "The woman you see is a dead woman, *s'abbocà*!" sobbed Tzia Rosina. She wept for a long time, in silence, drawing a small, immaculate handkerchief from the sleeve of her black blouse. This son of hers was an angel. That was all she managed to stammer out. That he was incapable of wrongdoing,

4

that he had always worked in service and no-one had ever had any complaint. Indeed his employers loved him like a son.

And in fact the testimony of Bartolomeo and Cosma Casùla Pes turned out to be, from this point of view, to all effects a paean of praise with regard to Zenobi. But they were upset that such a breach of faith – nine lambs stolen and sold for New Year's Day snacks, *spuntini de sa prima die 'e s'annu*, as they put it – had been wrought on them by the very one of their farmhands whom they trusted the most. The one who could come into the house and help himself to something to eat if he was hungry, who didn't even have to ask "may I?" or "do you mind?" or anything of the sort.

* * *

And then there was the matter of Sisinnia, because it was common knowledge that the two young people were attracted to one another. He's a handsome lad, but she's a dainty little Madonna, delicate as a piece of porcelain, they said. And moreover it seems that Cosma Casùla Pes, her father, was not all that unhappy about this attachment even though Sisinnia was only seventeen and Zenobi was already twenty-four. Those are not differences that matter: if the man is a little older, perhaps so much the better. Nothing official, far from it, because she had scarcely had a chance to look at him, so closely was she chaperoned every moment of the day.

She had these green eyes, Sisinnia had, and raven-black hair. Nor had she any lack of suitors, and indeed advantageous offers of marriage. A landowner from Orgòsolo, for example. A man hard put to it to reckon up all the property he had, recently left a widower, who after the minimal period of mourning had presented himself at the door of the Casùla Pes with a proposal of matrimony. But that did not come off, because the man was too advanced in years, and Sisinnia would have none of it and said outright: "Over my dead body!"

Her father could deny her nothing. Partly for this reason, perhaps, and in view of the attachment between the young people, he did not mention the fact that she was by no means indifferent to Zenobi. And it has to be said that in our part of the world a man who is too good-looking is viewed with suspicion, whereas a woman can never be too beautiful. However, the thing could be managed by taking the right steps: talking to her father, asking permission to meet, spending time together (though never alone!), and eventually there might emerge a regular betrothal.

It was at this point that the troubles started – and understand them who may.

However, "to get into such trouble just for a few lambs!" said Tzia Rosina. This was no work of Zenobi's.

6

Anyone could tell you that. They wanted to get him out of the way. Who knows, maybe someone else who had set eyes on the beauty of Sisinnia.

Maybe it was even her mother, Dolores Casùla Pes, who turned her nose up at the mere idea of such a marriage.

Not that Donna Dolores herself had been anything much before her own marriage: her mother was a maid-servant in the Siotto family, a hired hand, not a whit grander than that. Her trousseau had been sewn for her by Donna Luigia Siotto with her own fingers, otherwise she'd have had nothing of her own, not so much as a tear to shed. Not least because her father had died in Africa, so it wasn't as if Dolores Casùla Pes, whose maiden name was Bussu, had come from any family to speak of . . .

"If nobody gives a thought to poor people, *s'abbocà* . . . It's not that we have much, but what we have is yours. What counts is to clear this matter up – this curse that has come upon us."

"I simply must talk to him face to face. Otherwise how can I do anything at all?"

"But . . . but he doesn't trust anyone. Even with me he just turns up without warning. *S'abbocà*, I'll ask him anything you want me to. You just see if with a bit of patience I can't persuade him to meet you."

7

. . . Tzia Rosa said that Zenobi was constantly edgy and upset in the days after the business of these lambs came up. It hurt his feelings that no-one had come forward to express doubts about his guilt. "That's not the problem at all!" he had said to his mother shortly before he decided to light out for the hills. In fact I found it hard to understand how things had turned out the way they had. Zenobi had been constantly employed by the Casùla Pes for six years, during which time his conduct seems to have been exemplary. So much so that only a couple of years before the robbery he was entrusted to bargain on his employers' behalf at the sheep market. He made a good deal, with the result that Zenobi could thereafter number ten of his own sheep grazing along with those of his employers. At the end of September he escorted his boss's wife and daughter to Lula, for the Novena of San Francesco, having prepared all the provisions for the parish hospice and seen to replenishing the stores every other day, five or six hours on horseback to get there, and the same back.

That may have been the turning point of the whole business. I can almost see Sisinnia and Zenobi, their eyes never actually meeting, but casting each other covert glances all the way. He on horseback with his blue jacket open on his shirtfront. She dressed all in white, like a bride, her head lowered but jolted by the movement of the ox-cart, and him bare-headed and his blond forelock brushing his brow to the rhythm of his horse's hooves. And Donna Dolores brooding and brooding, *ca no est tonta* – that girl is no fool – she was saying to herself.

* * *

"I must think it over. You must realize that you are asking me to act tied hand and foot. And then, my dear lady, it has taken you seven months to make a move!"

"It seemed to be all arranged, *s'abbocà*. At first they said the whole thing could be settled by paying a fine. But who's going to convince Zenobi of that!"

"I must think it over. Come back this afternoon and we'll see."

"What about after you've had your lunch, *s'abbocà*?"

"No, rather later, about five o'clock if you can manage that. After lunch I take a walk to help me to think more clearly."

"May the Lord enlighten you, *s'abbocà*! Five o'clock, then?"

"At five, that'll do very well . . . "

* * *

So after lunch he set off for Biscollai, which in those days was a good step out of town. What time it was – before one o'clock – is certain and avouched for. Tzia Nevina, who was hanging out her washing at the very moment

9

when Bustianu passed by, had made him a gesture of respect and greeting, and then, as she was a bit on the chatty side, she even addressed him: "What, you, *s'abbocà*, abroad at this hour?"

Hot it was, my father told me, hot enough to roast any man alive who set foot on the road. This was the reason for Tzia Nevina's concern, though she was a woman who knew how to mind her own business. But Bustianu – he was one in a million – just put two fingers to his hatbrim by way of greeting, she tells us, and went his way without a word of explanation.

As to what the stakes were, this my father knew, because that very morning, right outside the courthouse, he had met Bustianu and stopped him in the street to ask him about some disputed bills that a cousin of his said had been paid but the Court said not. So he asked his advice as a lawyer. Bustianu told him to come back next day, he must make enquiries, because that was a matter for civil law whereas he only took on criminal cases. He also said that they couldn't meet until the following day, because he was busy that afternoon. He was going to take a walk towards Biscollai, as he had an important decision to come to. Whereupon my father asked him to name a time when it was convenient for him to call, even the day after, perhaps after lunch, and Bustianu said at once that after lunch was not a good hour, because that was when he took his daily walk, his "ever belovèd", as he called it.

Now, as long as you were only strolling in that direction you could do it on foot, but if you were aiming to go all the way up through the pass and reach the summit you had to do at least part of it on horseback, seeing there weren't any automobiles in those days, but once you were up there you could walk your legs off, there was no lack of space.

But that afternoon Bustianu didn't take a horse at all. Otherwise what would be so special about this walk? Answer me that!

So in short off he goes about his own business as he does every day after lunch, in a murderous heat. Not that this was any novelty, everyone knew he had this habit, even Tzia Nevina, who had no cause for surprise, except that it was a known thing that he took his "ever belovèd" in the direction of Sant'Onofrio, and to get to Sant' Onofrio he wouldn't have had to pass Tzia Nevina's house . . . So justification she did have, even if it was all up to him, God bless him!

* * *

. . . So I went on without any apparent destination. Just to stretch my legs. And I was glad that under that blazing sun, when even the dogs in the yards were curled up nice and comfy in the shade, there was not a soul stirring abroad. As if three in the afternoon had been three at night. Except for the light. Fierce and terrific it was, etching my shadow on the flagstones with a firm hand in the blackest Indian ink. The parched smell of the countryside was also a pleasure to me: the odours of cork-bark and ferula and mastic.

It was worth putting up with the heat, I can tell you. All the more so as I made my way down the slope, and thereafter upwards, upwards to the cool, as if the air itself beckoned me towards the hilltop with its promise of a refreshing breeze. And the sky, almost white above the heat-vibrant houses in Via Majore and in Séuna, once across the Iron Bridge, from Istiritta onwards, grew an ever deeper blue.

Not a cloud to be seen: it was so utterly dry that the cistus leaves dripped oil, while scarcely beyond the last buildings the withered brushwood and thistles crunched underfoot. No point in making cheese, I thought, for it would simply sweat and crack and sour. Not to speak of ricotta, which went off at once. In fact it was as hot as hell. Not that the rest of the year, a windy autumn, a bitter winter and a springtime laden with hailstorms, had been anything to write home about. The myrtle berries, which should have been as shiny and plump as dung-beetles, had shrivelled on the bushes. And the olive crop had been wretched, with fruit as pitiful and wizened black as sheep-droppings, and so devilish bitter that sacking them up was just a waste of time. And now it was merciless. With drains that tainted the motionless air and bluebottles gathered in seething swarms on the corpses of cats and dogs and crows. Only the laundry had the blessing of it, chalk-white, mashed up in boilers with soda and ashes and hung out in the back yards to dry. That is, when they could scrounge enough water to rinse it out, for the springwater down there at the washing-tubs had dwindled to a trickle as tiny as the trail of a snail.

Not a few back yards, what's more, gave off a sweetish, pungent whiff of meat cured with cumin, the guts of a lamb, a calf, a sheep, left there to fester while the Dog Star raged. And puffs of greasy smoke from the bread-ovens with their thick coatings of glazed soot.

Such was that afternoon, identical to the afternoons of summers past and those to come in this part of the world that they call a plateau, but is more of a bowl at the bottom of which live six or seven thousand souls, with the Cathedral and the Lawcourts practically cheek by jowl.

A bowl fringed around with all that is most unimaginably beautiful, with rock and thick moss, as curly and shaggy as an Ethiope's beard, with ilexes and sapling oaks and juniper and arbutus. With wild fennel and chicory, ferula and cardoons. With touches of silver and ochre and every conceivable nuance of green.

The beauty of it smites the eyes at last, and the nostrils, the lungs, the ears of me . . .

I don't know exactly why that afternoon I decided to change my route. I only know that once again I yearned to pursue that beauty, to reach it, and in so doing to flee the overwhelming heat. To flee that utter, catatonic silence, to flee the broiling "plateau" of granite slabs and the rust-coloured dust that fouled the air, to attain to the wonderworld of colour, the drilling din of the crickets, the breeze that fondled the life of each and every plant.

Maybe that afternoon I was feeling strong enough and mad enough to plan not so much a stroll as a real hike. For a hike it was, in view of my bulk, in view of the heat, and seeing that I hadn't brought the horse.

Maybe I felt a real need to take more time, to cover more ground, to break with routine.

I knew in my heart that I had to make an important decision, even if there was nothing to suggest that it might be a case any different from so many others. So I said, let's have a change today and go to Biscollai. So I said to myself.

I've always been one of those who talk to themselves. Yes, sir. Even if there are times when it's not a good thing. And I tell myself, "Enough of that, Bustianu! Now you're going too far." And then I remind myself of what my mother keeps telling me: "If it wasn't that you fought against yourself, my son, you'd have no enemies at all!" Ah, it was true! She meant I was too

14

austere, in a word, that I expected too much. And I had my settled habits. Such as going out walking after lunch, summer and winter, in sunshine or snow. As the Germans say: after lunch take an hour's sleep or a thousand paces. I had chosen the thousand paces. I put on my leggings and my hat, and took a stout stick, peeled and smooth and white as a bone, because going walking without a stick I seem to tire more quickly. Besides, it seemed to me that what that landscape, my landscape, needed was people for whom walking was – how shall I put it? – a ritual. Ancient hermits unsteady on their feet, blind bards wafting the air before them as they swing their staffs . . .

I will tell you a secret: I was led by my sense of smell. Almost entirely by that, while my pupils strove to find a gap through the slits of my eyelids, half shut to protect my eyes from the glare. And what my eyelids failed to do was done by the floppy brim of my hat, white in summer, dark in winter, and pulled down onto my nose. I was a kind of surface-going mole, sniffing out its territory. An old habit-bound donkey plodding along and asking no questions. And perhaps the real secret, the one that mattered, is simply that as I walked, leaning on the stick that I planted at least a step ahead of me, my brain stopped asking itself too many questions.

* * *

In short, he agreed to defend him, but the case was not easy, far from it. All the worse because at the beginning, months before, when agreement seemed to have been reached between the parties, Zenobi had gone into hiding. So that was that. If only he hadn't. Not much to be done about it now: he had guilt written all over him.

He says that they had been on the point of reaching this agreement, the Casùla Pes and Zenobi Sanna, who at the outset seemed willing enough. And the agreement was that Zenobi should pay the price of the vanished lambs plus a fine amounting to the tidy sum of a hundred lire, which today sounds like nothing but in those days was a lot of money. Considering that the entire value of the lambs was more or less twenty lire.

The agreement seemed reached, everything looked settled. If Zenobi paid up he wouldn't have to go to prison.

* * *

"It wasn't the money, *s'abbocà*. Because thank the Lord we have a little put by. It wasn't because of the hundred lire."

"Why was it, then?"

"You know why as well as I do. If he paid up it'd mean he'd committed the crime."

"And so instead he'll be committed to prison! Trying

16

to improve matters you've made them worse, do you realize that?"

"Perhaps prison was better. Because even if he paid he would be punished: they'd no longer go on employing him. And besides . . . "

"Besides?"

"And besides . . . you already know."

"You mean Sisinnia?"

"Yes, Sisinnia. That was what they were out to do: to break the bond between those two. Because they didn't think my son worthy of a Casùla Pes, you see – when they should have been licking their fingers at the prospect of such a son-in-law. He was too good for them. That's why they destroyed him, *s'abbocà*!"

"Why didn't you speak out at once then?"

"He wouldn't have it, he didn't want Sisinnia to be so much as mentioned. In any case on the night of the theft Zenobi wasn't even in Nùoro. He stole no lambs."

"Well then, if he wasn't in Nùoro where was he?"

"Who knows?"

"We won't get anywhere like this. You've got to trust me, otherwise how can I move a step?"

"*S'abbocà*, on the soul of my husband, wherever he may be in heaven, I swear I do not know. Zenobi is young, he's in the flower of his youth . . . "

"So how do you come to be so sure?"

"He is my son. I know him like the back of my hand.

17

When I tell you about him it's as if I were speaking of myself. He told me he was not in Nùoro. That means he was not in Nùoro. Anyway, I found this in his haversack while I was putting in some fresh bread."

"What is it?"

"*Itte chieres chi bos nia*? Don't ask me! I've brought it to you, *s'abbocà*. I can't read . . . "

2

BACHISIO LECCIS
Travelling photographer
Lifelike portraits at bargain prices!
Home delivery within thirty days!
Studio: Via della Pietà 36, Ozieri (Sassari)
FIVE LIRE

On the back, written in pencil, were the letters AQB and the number 29. Better than nothing. Perhaps irrelevant, but worth looking into. I applied to the police, to Sergeant Poli of the Carabinieri, a respectable, well-mannered person. He told me there was no mention of the photograph anywhere in the file, but that in his opinion it had no bearing on the case. I was not so sure. Maybe it could help me to prove that Zenobi was not in Nùoro on the night of the theft. I asked for a check-up on the trading licences for the month of December, to see if the photographer had also come to our parts, around Nùoro. The sergeant gave me a wry smile: "Trading licences?" He found this hilarious.

* * *

Permits — I ask you! In that respect, nothing has changed from that day to this, I'm sorry to say. Everyone does as he likes. If not worse. They don't apply for a permit even to build a house, so d'you expect them to when they want to take a couple of measly photographs? Nothing's changed, I say. The sergeant was tickled pink, you can be sure. However, he was fairly certain that no travelling photographers had come to Nùoro at that time.

Bustianu was not the man to give up, if there was a photograph he wanted to see it. What's more, he wanted a firm date, it had become a matter of principle. The fact was that he believed Tzia Rosina — she reminded him of his own mother to a T. This is how things go at times, maybe if there hadn't been that resemblance he wouldn't have been so bloody-minded about it . . .

* * *

. . . And then there were questions I didn't manage to fathom. Nothing seemed to hang together. Number One: Zenobi had no need to steal those lambs. Two:

20

given a little patience he might even have been able to marry Sisinnia. Three: he had solid prospects. Four: he was a decent young man, modest in his ways and well regarded. Five: unexpectedly one evening he leaves Nùoro for God knows where. Six: the night following his departure nine lambs are stolen from the Casùla Pes's sheepfold at Marreri. Seven: lambs worth only nineteen or twenty lire. Only nine out of a hundred and fifty: that makes number eight. The very same night the Carabinieri call on Tzia Rosina asking for her son. That's nine. She says he is not there, that he's been away since the previous day but she doesn't know where. Which makes ten.

Everything more or less straightforward. In fact, perfectly so. How was it therefore that Zenobi chose to take to the hills? All the more so because the risk was serious: he became guilty by default. Going on the run, which looks disastrously like an admission of guilt. With the Casùla Pes's attempt to reach a settlement with him, that put them in the right – only to have this thrown in their face by the one of all their farmhands whom they trusted the most. It would mean a verdict of guilty with knobs on. Unless Zenobi gave himself up.

"I have to meet him! As things stand my hands are tied, in court they won't even let me open my mouth. Don't you understand?"

Tzia Rosina sat there with lowered head. She understood, she understood all too well. But who would talk the boy round? If Zenobi got a bee in his bonnet it was no good pressing him. That's the way he'd always been. Growing up without a father, that was the reason for it. Because a father always knows what has to be done and when.

"You've got to persuade him to meet me. Wherever he wants, but soon. We're running out of time."

And Tzia Rosina started to sob and say she didn't know when he would turn up; that he came by night, without warning; that there was a great hand crushing her heart and her very bowels; that sleep had been out of the question ever since this disaster had occurred; that her son was scared and trusted no-one; that the Casùla Pes were a power in the land.

"I am bound to absolute secrecy, you realize? You realize that I can do nothing to the injury of a client of mine? You must tell him that. When he chooses, where he chooses."

And she went on dabbing at her nose with a handkerchief already irremediably shredded. Yes she would tell him, as soon as ever she could, but she wouldn't make any promises. She knew what Zenobi was like.

* * *

A week before the hearing Bustianu said he was going

to visit an old friend in Ozieri. So he took the 7.35 train from Nùoro. To reach Ozieri he had to change at Tirso, a station out in the open country. A half-hour wait, from 9.19 to 9.50. If all went well he would arrive at half-past two. In fact he got to Ozieri in the late afternoon. And there he found the catastrophe awaiting him. To cut a long story short, the photographer was dead. In a fire that had destroyed his studio forty-eight hours previously.

In Ozieri there was a certain Sergeant Tuvoni of the Royal Guard, a tubby little man with a handlebar moustache. In his opinion the case already had a name plastered all over it: Zenobi Sanna, fugitive from justice.

This was a blow for Bustianu. He decided to go and talk to this sergeant, and got a sceptical reception.

* * *

He received me in his office in the barracks with the air of one about to grill a suspect. He was sarcastic about my being in Ozieri so soon that it could scarcely be accidental. I justified myself by pleading personal reasons for my presence, but his little black eyes evinced nothing but more scepticism. I asked for information about what had happened. He confined himself to telling me what I already knew. Two nights previously a fire had destroyed the Leccis studio with its owner inside it. From the charred remains it was clear that Leccis had been surprised by the flames while at work in the darkroom

23

itself. Nothing had survived the destruction, not a ledger, not a photographic plate, not a receipt. Whoever had started the blaze was out to eliminate an awkward witness. But witness to what?

* * *

"You keep writing all this stuff in our newspapers about these felons, maybe you'll understand the problems we have to overcome without your creating a sort of legendary aura, so to speak, around these bandits." Not wishing to sink to that level Bustianu decided to hold his peace. Sergeant Tuvoni fell silent for a moment or two, then continued: "It is not surprising that the common people don't collaborate, when even educated persons, poets, writers, men of law, do nothing but applaud the exploits of those who deliberately set themselves against the State. Against the Established Order." More silence. Bustianu had noted how emphatically he had stressed the words "State" and "Established Order". "If we get no collaboration from persons of influence in our community, how can we expect collaboration from the unlettered, the illiterate?" He had done his homework, had the sergeant. "But anyway, what is it you people say? Power to the proletariat!"

"Bread for everyone! That's what we say!" burst out Bustianu. "A few crumbs for those who make the bread, that at least! But we're not here to talk politics.

I am here officially to ask what are the charges against my client."

"Arson and first degree homicide as well as robbery and misappropriation . . . need I go on?" replied the sergeant without turning a hair.

"I see no connection between my client and Leccis," said Bustianu, chancing his arm.

The sergeant gave him an apparently affable smile. He leafed in leisurely fashion through a pile of papers on his desk. "I have here the record of an exchange of letters with Sergeant Poli of the Nùoro Carabinieri informing me of what I should call an extremely close connection between your client and the photographer."

Bustianu tugged angrily at his beard: he had supplied that connection himself! "At that rate," he said, striving to appear perfectly calm, "we would have to suspect anyone else who had their photograph taken by Leccis. Anyone might have had something to hide."

"How right you are, Avvocato, how right you are! There's nowhere in the world with more things to hide than here!"

"The fact seems to me circumstantial," resumed Bustianu, holding up a cigar to ask permission to light it.

"In a court of law, perhaps, Avvocato," smirked Sergeant Tuvoni, giving a nod as if to concede the permission requested. "But we are simple labouring men, we do the dirty work outside the lawcourts, Avvocato, whatever the weather, at every hour of day or night, so we don't have all that much time for quibbles."

At this point Bustianu began to lose patience. He made a lot of noise puffing out the smoke so as to mask his rising temper. "There are no quibbles here. Not in this case. Even if some measure of attention to the details of the matter would not come amiss to a person claiming to administer justice."

"What d'you mean by that?" It was the sergeant's turn to lose his temper. "Do you suggest that I should allow you to thwart all our efforts, to let all those rogues go free, to make heroes of them? I'd like to see you crawling on hands and knees into every nook and cranny. What price quibbles then?"

"But these are nothing but rumours, Sergeant, and consequently I can only presume that you have nothing in hand with which to bring charges against my client."

The sergeant went purple in the face. "What sort of civilization is this?" he thundered. "How can we claim to be admitted to human society if all the tremendous toil forced upon us day by day is reduced to nothing in the Courts of Law?"

"No-one is exempt, Sergeant, there are connivances here there and everywhere. The mayor, the parish priest, the local M.P., even the military: we are all bound as you are to serve that blindfold lady with the scales of Justice. Moreover we have to fight against prejudice, against sentences pronounced before a case comes to trial, against this mania for shooting first and asking questions afterwards, against this dangerous tendency to make no distinctions. This, I fear, is what sets us apart from human society, as you put it. However, it is late, and I think I have taken up too much of your time," concluded Bustianu as he got to his feet. He was fatigued and frustrated.

He had all but reached the door when the sergeant stopped him in his tracks. "A price has been put on your client's head," he announced at the very moment when Bustianu's hand touched the doorhandle. "Two thousand lire."

So he had become an outlaw. A bloodthirsty beast in the eyes of all. Zenobi Sanna had entered the ranks of those who cause old women to cross themselves at the mere mention of his name.

What years those were! And then they go talking about "The Athens of Sardinia". Wild West, more like! You scarcely had time to poke your head out than along came a bullet from the blue. Because you had seen something without knowing it. Because you had happened to hear something you ought not to have heard. Or merely because you worked for someone who was on the black list. In a word, life was cheap.

An uncle of mine, or to be precise a great-uncle, he

being my grandfather's younger brother, nearly came to a sticky end that way, for when he was out hunting for mushrooms he found himself faced by a band of armed men. He was a peace-loving fellow with no experience of weapons. At a certain point he approached a spring of water to get a drink and saw a bunch of men sitting round it. Men with guns. Hunters, he thought, and carried on regardless. Then a stocky character, not wearing a Sardinian cap, with a nasty expression, two sharp snake-eyes and a moustache that looked fake on his baby-face, left the group, strode towards him and asked where he was going. My uncle replied that he was thirsty, that he was hunting for mushrooms because it had been raining for two days, and so on. The other told him there were no mushrooms thereabouts, that the water in that spring was not fit to drink, and that he should look elsewhere.

It was Berrina, ladies and gentlemen, the worst bandit in circulation. He jabbed his shotgun into my uncle's belly and told him to run along home, that they had never so much as set eyes on each other. My uncle turned himself around and couldn't get home fast enough. He was in such a fit of trembling that he went straight to bed with a high fever and diarrhoea. He felt obliged to pay for a Mass at the Madonna delle Grazie, since Berrina had been in a good mood and perhaps was there simply to stock up with water and not up to anything in particular. Otherwise my grandfather's brother would not only have never seen his home again, but they wouldn't even have been able to take him to *sa'e* Manca and bury him. Not that it happens all that often that an empty coffin is buried.

But to come back to Bustianu, he returns from Ozieri to find things looking blacker and blacker for Zenobi. Nor can he get anything out of Tzia Rosina, for all she can do is weep, poor woman! Meanwhile for the business with the lambs the sentence handed down is very harsh: six years' imprisonment, by default.

And the months pass . . .

3

THE THIRTEENTH OF NOVEMBER, TO THE DAY. ALMOST
a year after the event. And I was off for my usual "ever
belovèd" towards Sant'Onofrio, which was my accus-
tomed goal. The weather was turning chilly, so I put on
a heavy cloak and the old felt hat I wear in the country.
I climb under the Seminary archway, give a passing
wave to the Law Courts, flank the Cathedral and then
off, off towards the scrublands and the young oaks and
the odour of sandalwood. I am crunching my way
over the acorns when I hear a rustling sound behind
me. Without looking back, I forge ahead towards the
summit, deeply inhaling the air which at every step
becomes more effervescent. A few bluish clouds are
hovering above the sheer bluffs overhanging Olíena.
Rain's on the way, I think. Though Mount Orthobene
is cloudless, the air is so clear, the landscape so limpid
that I seem to be living within the very source of light.

Green things are liquor-clear, brown things are aglow, the grey of the granite shimmers with a silvery light. It occurs to me that this would not suit our painter Antonio Ballero, this crystal light would not be to his taste. Because his palette is as murky as barley water when he mixes his whites, like soot for his blacks, and for his reds like leaping flames. And his brush is too muted for this landscape of pitiless, intolerable dazzle. I am turning over these thoughts when with the rustling behind me comes the snap of a twig underfoot. I turn round with a start.

* * *

"Sisinnia?" asks Bustianu, eyeing the slender figure that has stiffened to a statue a few steps behind him.

She makes a gesture of assent: yes, it is herself indeed. Her face is a perfect, pure-white oval framed, as it were, by the delicate dun-coloured kerchief surrounding it. Hers is a beauty quite out of the ordinary, even disproportionate in the full lips that seem stamped in vivid red on the immaculate ivory face, in the deep green eyes, as round and liquid as those of a young calf, in the shapely brow onto which fall a few raven, almost blue-black locks escaped from her kerchief. Everything about her is sweetness without frailty, beauty without affectation. "Sisinnia," repeats Bustianu with the suggestion of a smile.

"Will I never see him again?" she asks in the ghost of

a voice, as she worries the black beads of a rosary hanging from her apron. She weeps without shedding a tear, her fine bosom heaving in time with her panting breath. "He wasn't even in Nùoro that night, he wasn't even here." This time she can hardly get the words out, her throat is choked with sobs.

Bustianu is at a loss what to say. "Child, why didn't you say so at once?" is the best he can come out with. And he thinks that this reproof so oft repeated, like the words of a psalm, makes this story into a story of silences. A story of things not said, though a simple, clear, straight-forward story it is.

Sisinnia shakes her head for a long time before speaking. "He didn't wish it," she says at last. "He preferred to go into hiding rather than . . . " And she is shaken with fresh sobs.

Bustianu takes a step towards her, stretches out a hand to lay on her shoulder. But Sisinnia backs away.

"If he doesn't show up there's nothing we can do," says Bustianu, attempting to force her to react.

"*He* knows who stole those lambs!" she blurts out all of a sudden.

Her tears have now ceased, her eyes are shining like uncut emerald, ringed around with a hint of cornelian. Her lips close in a resounding silence.

"Who was it?" demands Bustianu. He gazes round as if wishing to return to the thoughts, the colours from which he has been torn, to Antonio Ballero and his palette . . .

"My father," she answers, almost in a whisper.

In short, Cosma Casùla Pes had put a good face on it when he realized that Sisinnia and Zenobi were attracted to one another, but he can't have been too pleased about it. So he prepared his little joke. To get rid of a possible son-in-law who was as poor as a church mouse but too good-looking. So he sends him out of Nùoro to a farm near Galtellì, miles and miles away, to see to a matter of some unbranded cattle. Awaiting him is the steward, a young man from Posada. The order is to check over the herd of some thirty head and brand them within forty-eight hours. Zenobi and the steward set to work . . .

"My child, you should have spoken out earlier!" sighs Bustianu again, but gently, so as not to further her wide-eyed stare of alarm. So frail does Sisinnia look that a single puff of wind would be enough to hurl her down over the bluff into the chasm below.

"I didn't know!" she protests. "I didn't know until now about Galtellì and the herd."

"And what about this steward from Posada? Who is he? We may still be in time." She sketches a smile. "He's someone I've only seen a couple of times. His name's Piredda. Luigi Piredda."

33

"Good. If the charge of robbery is disproved, every-thing will be easier."

"We are in your hands," murmurs Sisinnia. Then she burrows under her apron as if to do something of great importance that has only just occurred to her. She draws out an envelope and offers it to him. "It's for you," she says.

Bustianu hesitates a second or two before reaching out to take it.

"What is it?" he asks, still undecided whether to accept it or not.

Sisinnia stands stock-still, with extended hand, holding the envelope. He will never forget that hand: whiter than the envelope itself, her fingernails a delicate pink and polished like coral beads. "I don't know. It's him who gave it to me to give to you," she murmurs as if abashed.

Bustianu takes the envelope, on which his name is written in bold, clear letters. He puts it in his pocket. It needs but a touch to tell him that it contains something bulky, not a mere sheet of paper.

To cut matters short his walk, his "ever belovèd", is ruined. Even the weather is turning nasty. So just as soon as the lass with brisk steps has vanished from his sight Bustianu makes his way back home. Every so often he pats his pocket to make sure the envelope is there. No doubt about it, this was one of those affairs you can see no way out of, the ones that play tricks on you. Because you think you are in control and instead, far from it! In my opinion Bustianu felt just this way, like someone who thinks he is cured of an illness and yet keeps on having relapses. As soon as he gets home, without even removing his cloak, he seizes the envelope, looks at it for a long time, at his name inscribed in fine rather sloping handwriting. At last he makes up his mind, opens it with a kitchen knife and extracts a photograph.

The gilt lettering at the bottom leaves no room for doubt: Leccis Photographic Studio, Via della Pietà 36, Ozieri, Sassari. The subject is a sturdy, fair-haired youngster gazing intently towards the photographer yet beyond the photographer. As if eager to escape from the frame and look into the eyes of whomever he had in his own mind's eye. There is no hint of diffidence about him, no nonsense about cameras catching your likeness and stealing your soul along with it. Not even the fear that the lens masks the barrel of a gun aimed straight at you. He is bareheaded, his black Sardinian stocking-cap slapped over his right shoulder, as if to stress the contrast with the whiteness of his face, the suggestion of golden down on his chin, and his long, luxurious locks tousled by a gentle breeze and shining like the sunrays of a monstrance. His irises are so pale that they almost shade off into the whites of his eyes, around sharp, jet black pupils. But this does not lessen the intensity of his gaze, or prevent it from seeing the landscape over which it is roving, or envisioning the woman afar off at whom he is directing it, or conceal the love which has so skilfully filled it with a grave sweetness. Zenobi Sanna has adopted the posture of a Mannerist angel, his arm slightly raised to rest his elbow on a plaster pillar, perhaps a fragment of an ancient ruin that had somehow ended up in those parts.

* * *

Beneath his dark waistcoat his white shirt, so white as to make a milky blur on the photograph, is fastened by two filigree buttons. But he is not wearing full local costume. From the waist down he is dressed like a middle-class country gentleman, his muscular legs clad in a pair of continental-style trousers, his calves enclosed in leggings fastened with straps. This mixture of dress has a strange effect on me. But it marks him out as a man divided, half in and half out, half Sardinian and half mainlander. That's it – split between tradition and the future. Not like me, who have seldom worn Sardinian costume. Who am what I have become: middle class, a graduate, a mainlander living on an island. Because I have crossed the sea, I have! And read books, perhaps too many. I have made a choice. Not so Zenobi. Who nevertheless wears drainpipe trousers such as are in the fashion and sold by tailors to the gentry. This perplexes me. Maybe he has picked up a message that I have missed. A message that gets across to the younger generations in spite of all. Despite the silence imposed by an overwhelming past, the very myth of its own self. Despite the shackles, despite the isolation of being . . . an islander.

This dual nature shakes me, it frightens me and I feel saddened, inadequate and guilty. I am only thirty and I feel an old man.

It is that figure which causes such feelings in me. It is what it means, what it is trying to convey to me. Time which changes things, even those that seem unchangeable. That changes ways of thinking, customs, certainties.

I place the photograph on the marble table-top. As if to abandon it to its fate. Three logs of seasoned oak are burning slowly in the fireplace, a fire that will stay in, dropping embers like uncut rubies, good for cooking lamb on.

Finally I take off my cloak.

I pick up the photograph again. The background, which appears to be a cloth hung between two trees, depicts a kind of Baroque entrance hall, with a glimpse of a curving staircase. The third dimension has vanished into the monochrome, out of focus. Only the subject himself is in focus, and vivid with it. Because that young man wants to live, to live his own life on his own terms, which are terms acceptable everywhere else, but not here in Nùoro.

I desperately want to talk to him, I want to look him straight in the eye, get him to explain what I have not understood.

If this village becomes a city, and sooner or later it will, I want to know exactly what city we have to plan for.

I don't much care for that grey blur in one top corner of the photograph, that fragment of a building which the faulty framing has fixed for ever beyond the painted curtain forming the backdrop. It looks like Reality, graphic, pleonastic, once more coming knocking at the door and crying: "Here I am! You have jested, you have built castles in the air, you have immortalized yourselves, but mine is a grey, sickly sky, with a fragment of a building: I have my own things to fix on the photographic plate. In this image of what would wish to be I am that which actually *is*."

I call to mind Francesco Ciusa when he accuses me of having a profoundly religious spirit. What, me? A religious spirit? I who am rationality personified? And what about him, who sculpts farmers' wives as if they were angels and shepherds like crucified Christs?

Of course if words are a religion, if justice is a religion, if the earth we tread is a religion, that's a different matter . . .

* * *

My father, who as I have told you knew him well, says that in the days that followed his meeting with Sisinnia

38

Bustianu was prickly, he had a bee in his bonnet. He could not resign himself to it, when he thought of that youngster who had gone on the run for no reason. Because Bustianu was not one to stand on ceremony, he came right out and said that among all these Robin Hood-type bandits there were also just plain criminals, scum who had found the easiest way to get what they wanted. The truth was that many of these were simply bullies, men who had no idea of what it meant to live on civilized terms with their neighbours. They were brute beasts, and that's the truth of it. Such who if something wasn't going their way expressed their opinions with a shotgun or a knife. That's the way it was! Nothing to swagger or brag about, far from it!

But not everyone had the same ideas.

And so by using these over-subtle arguments, by looking for difficulties in short, by trying to consider each case on its merits, Bustianu passed for a man who wrote poems about the Robin-Hood myth. I ask you, what a myth! Read what Bustianu himself wrote, and read it with care! Some myth, I say! Some Athens of Sardinia! Luckless folk, o yes, you can say *that* again.

4

"I THINK THAT DISTINCTIONS HAVE TO BE MADE, I REALLY do!" One might have called Bustianu's tone peremptory.

Sergeant Poli handed him another glass of malmsey wine.

"By making distinctions, as you put it, one runs the risk of finding oneself up a gum tree. People here have to understand that if they go along with these scoundrels they have put themselves on the wrong side of the law. They must understand that they are now part of a nation, they are Italians, in short that they are not the only pebbles on the beach."

"And who tells them so? The Piedmontese army? Or the king's royal tax-collectors?" Bustianu's questions hung in the air of the salon of the Café Tettamanzi.

"Don't come the Populist over me now, you understood exactly what I meant to say," said the sergeant, ignoring the questions. "You are Sardinian yourself, and a decent person. It's a question of deciding and accepting one's own responsibilities."

"There are lots of decent people to be sure, even around these parts, people who may have already decided in their own hearts but do not have sufficient say. You cannot go on judging the many who have no say by the few who kick up all the row."

"Kick it up they certainly do, their hullabaloo even reaches Rome," agreed the sergeant. "And now at H.Q. they're talking about sending whole divisions over here, about emergency measures. Our orders are clear in this respect: don't be over-scrupulous: shoot first!"

"Exactly. That's just what I meant about making distinctions. You shoot first: and we have the scruples. But in any case we get by with our scruples."

"And a fat lot of good they do, your scruples! Eyewitnesses who forget as if by magic before their official deposition, who vanish just before they are due to go into court."

"They're scared, they know that Rome is far, far away."

"So you make excuses for them?"

"I understand them. By no means do I make excuses for them. But exploiting hunger and insecurity to sway the people cannot lead to any lasting results. This is not a territory like any other. None of them are. Take your own case, Sergeant. When you opened the letter posting you to this place stuck out in the middle of the sea didn't you think: 'What have I done? Why are they punishing me? Why are they packing me off to live among savages?' You see what a long way we have to go? We are not just any old citizens, we are not Italians like the rest of you. We are beasts of burden and dogs of war."

"You tell me this . . . "

"But have you any idea what this place was like? And these people? How can one expect them to understand if no-one explains?"

"Avvocato, with this talk of explaining it looks to me as if you're all having us on. I mean that when you wish to do so you understand at once."

"One thing we grasped at once and without any need to have it explained to us. Namely, that what we are, what we have been, and what we will be, doesn't matter a damn to anybody."

"And why so? It's the usual moan. After all, your representatives in Parliament were scarcely elected by us!"

"*Touché*! However I am consoled by the fact that I didn't vote for them. Shall we have another?" suggested Bustianu waving his empty glass in the direction of the waiter. "And so," he continued, changing the subject, "His Majesty's Prosecutor is leaving us . . . "

"So it seems," replied the sergeant laconically, sniffing at the malmsey just poured out for him. They drank in silence for a while, then he added, "We are expecting a great farewell reception in honour of His Excellency His Majesty's Prosecutor. Something on a grand scale. This party is being flung by Avvocato Mastino and consort, with guests from Sassari and Cagliari, officials, delegates, mayors ... You will be there yourself, I understand."

"So it seems." Bustianu echoed the sergeant's words with a shrug.

It was at that moment that Corporal Cugusi of the Carabinieri appeared in the glare of the doorway, contracting his brows as he peered into the dimness in search of his superior. For Sergeant Poli, who had his back to the entrance, it was enough to see that Bustianu's expression changed, and that he was making signs to someone behind him, to realize that his work-break was over. He turned, saw Cugusi, and beckoned to him. The latter sprang to obey, threading his way between the tables. He saluted, and confined himself to saying "Cosma Casùla Pes." Adding only: "At Marreri."

And thus they found him, apparently asleep at the foot of a wild olive tree, his gun propped up against the trunk. He had been shot at close quarters. His white shirt was reduced to a mush of red gore from breastbone to throat. Beneath the yellowish skin the flesh was ripped open like crimson velvet. The ground on every side of him was soaked by abundant streams of blood.

Sergeant Poli elbowed his way through the small

43

crowd that had collected round the body. Two carabinieri gave him a brief summary: it was the daughter
who had alerted them.

They had been together, Cosma and Sisinnia, looking
over the farm, fondling the almonds on the trees, gath-
ering a little chicory and wild fennel. While he was
about it, Cosma had brought his gun along, on the
chance of bagging a hare or two. Sisinnia had had a picnic
prepared: salted meat, bread made from bran, sheep's
cheese, a chunk of dried sausage, a flask of good wine.
She enjoyed these excursions to Marreri, and Cosma had
got into the habit of taking her with him. The farmhands
were a long way off, in the sheep-fold curdling the
milk and making rush baskets to drain it. The girl had
slipped off on her own for a few minutes to fill her apron
with chicory and cardoons. Then she heard a shot. He's
bagged a hare, she thought, as she pushed aside a clump
of brambles which hid a handful of wild asparagus. So she
made her way back to the giant wild olive quite calmly.
And she found him on the ground. As if asleep. Not a
dead hare in sight. But blood, rivers of it.

Sergeant Poli gave Bustianu a meaning look. "He's
done for himself this time," he said. "What's the phrase
here? He's pissed and missed the potty."

Bustianu raised a hand to his brow as if to protect his
eyes from too fierce a light. "Not so fast, Sergeant," he
said, thinking hard.

"He bumped him off. He bumped him off while he was asleep. It's obvious."

They had trouble shifting the onlookers, shepherds grazing flocks nearby, the farmhands, the municipal agricultural expert, all sorts of people. Nevertheless, not one of them had seen a thing. A fleeting shadow, a fugitive. None of them had set eyes on Zenobi in the neighbourhood. From Sisinnia they obtained nothing more than what she had already told. Her face spoke of terror and desperation. Bustianu gazed at her for a long time, while her hands never ceased to worry her black-beaded rosary.

Moving the corpse was no easy matter either. The victim's head was hanging down, attached to his body by a mere strip of flesh. They laid him on an improvised stretcher to transport him to the police station. Sisinnia followed these operations in a kind of impassive turmoil. Her face had gone chalk-white and her eyes were fixed in a vacant stare into the remotest distance . . . Eyes of a frightened gazelle or a wild beast ready to spring.

"He wasn't killed in his sleep," said Bustianu, approaching the great olive tree but careful not to tread near where Cosma had fallen.

"You see here?" he asked the sergeant, following close behind him. Poli turned to the part of the trunk Bustianu was pointing at. It was about a metre and a half from the ground. Hundreds of pellets had penetrated the wood, giving the effect of a piece of old furniture attacked by woodworm. Tiny spatters of blood and flesh had stained the bark.

Sergeant Poli picked up the gun, opened it, nodded.

"Yes, it's been fired," he said.

"He was on his feet when they shot him," concluded Bustianu.

"Even if that were so," returned the sergeant, "it wouldn't change matters."

"It does change them, substantially," reflected Bustianu.

"I am waiting to hear your opinion," said Sergeant Poli with a touch of pique.

Bustianu took a few steps away from the tree. "Nothing makes sense to me, Sergeant," he said at length. "Why shoot him?"

The sergeant smiled faintly. "What a question! To kill him . . . "

"Yes, yes, of course! That's clear enough. But why shoot him with his own gun?"

"Perhaps your client had no weapon with him."

"What, a fugitive from justice, and bloodthirsty at that, going around without a weapon? No-one has ever seen an unarmed bandit!"

"He wasn't to know he would meet his sworn enemy. Casùla Pes probably put down his gun for some reason and Sanna seized his chance. Most likely the victim had decided to take a rest in the shade of the tree and Sanna took him by surprise."

"Yes, he just happened to see him, went up so close as to take his gun, then backed off far enough to be able to shoot. Come off it, Sergeant!"

"You make it all too complicated, but the situation is as clear as daylight. Casùla Pes had nodded off and Sanna shot him dead with no trouble at all. *Sic et simpliciter.*"

"And he didn't use his own gun? Or a knife? It would have been easier, cleaner, not so noisy. Better in every way. Plus the risk of being seen, being captured, and, what is even more incredible, the risk of being shot himself."

"Only because you start from the assumption that the victim was not asleep."

"He was not asleep. The shot was too high. Cosma Casùla Pes slipped down into the position in which he was found."

"You are therefore a ballistics expert?"

"Not really, but I've seen quite a few corpses. And I'm willing to bet you as much as you like that Cosma Casùla Pes was standing up when he was shot. Then there's another thing . . . " Bustianu paused.

Sergeant Poli lowered his eyelids slightly, gave a nod, and confined himself to murmuring, "Go on."

"Zenobi Sanna is a crack shot, he could have killed him with perfect ease from fifty paces away. Whereas . . . "

"He might not have had his gun with him!" The sergeant's voice betrayed a certain amount of agitation, he was now obviously in some doubt.

"Whereas," continued Bustianu, refusing to be side-tracked, "whereas he approached dangerously close. Cosma Casùla Pes was a crack shot himself. It would have been a terrific risk."

"Not if he was asleep!" burst out the sergeant. "We're wasting time making improbable conjectures, Avvocato. And you know better than I do the way these people's minds work. He wanted to be seen while he was killing him, perhaps he wanted to say something, he wanted ... "

5

SO HE WANTED TO MAKE HIM PAY FOR IT! POLI might be right.

The sergeant gave me a stare as if a gulf had suddenly yawned open between us. I had become a Sardinian, a conniver, someone unable to think straight. The decent person I had been until then was changing before his eyes into a shady lawyer, into a pettifogger prepared to justify a criminal. Prepared to go to any lengths to save his own client. Apart from the fact that, technically, Zenobi Sanna could not be held to be my client. I had never met him. All I knew about him I had learnt from his mother. The only picture I had of him was a photograph which did not exonerate him from anything. Indeed, on the contrary, it forged the strongest possible link between him and the murdered photographer Leccis.

There was another thing I knew, and it was no small matter: Sisinnia had revealed to me that it had been none other than her father, Cosma Casùla Pes, also murdered, who had organized the little trick with the lambs which had cost Zenobi Sanna a sentence of six years' imprisonment.

Therefore the sergeant was right, I was bending over backwards so as not to admit that my client, as he called him, was nothing but a bloodthirsty beast, a criminal who deserved no indulgence whatever, a dangerous fugitive from justice who had tasted the blood of his enemies, a savage unfit for human society. A wild animal to be killed on sight.

And yet he was wrong!

Have you ever had an absolute certainty with nothing to back it up? A certainty that grows all the more certain the more appearances are against it?

That's how it was with me! Maybe it was due to his mother, Tzia Rosina, and what she said: "I know my son." But how many mothers say that! Or maybe from Zenobi's face in the photograph, as he gazed into space. Like Carjat's portrait of Rimbaud. Though Zenobi had reached the age of twenty-four without ever writing a poem. Maybe it was Sisinnia's eyes, that shone at the mere mention of his name.

There, I am made that way: obstinate, a typical man of the Barbagia. It must mean something to be born in one place rather than another.

I am not talking about any doctrine of innate ideas.

I believe that one's place of birth is pure geographical chance, the outcome a matter for the registry-office. But that said, growing up in one place rather than another surely must be of some consequence. Because of the air, perhaps, or the landscape, who knows? It may be that if you grow up in the plains, among the mists, you learn to appreciate nuances, to nurture a sense of relativity. It may be that if you are born in a place without mountains, in the midst of the hurly-burly, it's easier for you to make concessions. I don't know. The fact is that I am made the way I am: when I get an idea into my head there's no-one can get it out again. I am worse than my dog, who at least, if I beat him, does what I tell him to. I can't even do that much. When I was in the army at Bologna I risked Court Martial twice. Not to speak of my student years in Sassari.

* * *

"Are you certain of what you say?" thundered Bustianu in overwrought tones. The old woman scrutinized him as one does something indecipherable. She attempted a smile. "Have you been listening carefully?" insisted Bustianu, gradually raising his voice. "Have you under-stood what I asked you?"

"I've understood, I've understood, I'm not deaf and I'm not even half-witted, thanks be to God!" cut in the old woman. "You've come all this way for nothing.

Luisi has gone away. To America, that's where he's gone. He wanted to take us with him, but Lenardu, my husband, he wouldn't hear of it. Speaking for myself I'd have gone, but Lenardu, no-one can budge him. What d'you expect me to say? When someone's seventy years old you can't expect him to change his spots from one day to the next. So Luisi took his family and his younger brother and they went off there to America. He says they'll write, they'll send money . . . "

Bustianu was sweating. In the humid heat of the Baronìa his clothes stuck to him like clingfilm. "To America," he repeated to himself out loud. "But perhaps you can help me all the same," he said hopefully. "About a year ago your son branded a number of head of cattle, cows and calves, belonging to his employer. A farmhand came down from Nùoro to help him, a fair-haired young man, you can't fail to have noticed him."

The woman looked once more at Bustianu. Her face now showed a trace of concern, as if she were disconcerted by the other's persistence. This lawyer who had travelled all the way from Nùoro to Galtellì just to talk to her son about things that had happened a year before. "What do you expect me to know about it, young man? Who can remember a job done so long ago?"

"Surely you must remember! A young man with fair hair and blue eyes, from Nùoro . . . the branding . . . " stammered Bustianu. And if the old dame had not been so minute he would have seized her by the shoulders and shaken out the words she didn't want to utter. But she didn't even glance at him. Seated on the stone step of her cottage, with its whitewashed drystone walls, she calmly went on shelling beans. From her lightweight skirt emerged two bare feet like overcooked buns and two swollen ankles, although winter was well advanced. "Give him back to his mother!" Bustianu made this last attempt. "He's become a fugitive although he is innocent."

"And what d'you expect me to do about it?" snapped the old woman, shelling beans without a pause. After long silence: "He's an outlaw, then?" she said, as if she had only at that moment grasped Bustianu's meaning.

He gave a vigorous nod, full of hope.

"Oh, they're all outlaws now," was her comment. "But the real outlaws, the ones who were on the side of the poor, they don't exist any more. When I was young it was a different matter. There were injustices, they had taken away our lands and pastures and everything else. I saw the Chiaragone brothers slaughtered like beasts, they didn't waste time putting people on trial. And they were honest folk. People who had lost everything when they enclosed the land. One of them, the youngest, was not even outlawed when they killed him. Injustice, young fellow, is as old as mankind."

"I agree, but you too, if you keep silent when you

53

could help justice, are an accomplice. Because you know who it is we are talking about."

"What am I supposed to tell you? You are young, and I was, we all were, folk with some schooling in those days, believe me. We weren't always the way we are now. What d'you think you're rummaging for, young man, things are the way they are, when you land up in the middle of . . . "

"In that case, if not even we make distinctions, we put the others in the right. You too put the beans in one place and the pods in another, because you can't eat them both together. The youngster I am speaking of is innocent and you have to help me." By this time an imploring note had crept into Bustianu's voice.

"I don't know what you're after, it's Luisi's business. Anyway, even the pods are good when there's nothing else to eat."

It was at this point that a man's voice was heard from inside the cottage.

The old dame smoothed down her hair and adjusted her kerchief. She waited a few seconds before answering the summons. "*Itte bata?*" she cried, turning towards the darkness behind her. "It's my husband," she explained to Bustianu. "He's ill, they say they're treating him but he gets worse and worse. We're in our second childhood, my lad. I must go inside now, and I can't even ask you to come in for a bite because we have nothing."

She got to her feet with an effort, picked up the bowl of beans and took the pods in her apron, held by the corners. "A handsome youngster, good and fresh in the face" she said on the threshold. "Wait here," she added.

When she came back out she had something in her hand.

Eh, heh! So there was another photograph. Taken at the farm by the same roving photographer. Bustianu practically had a fit. It showed Zenobi with the branding iron in his hand and Luigi Piredda holding a calf by its head. It showed a grey building in the near distance. The same which had been partly hidden in the background of Zenobi's portrait. There was other information to be gleaned from that photograph, but the most important was the handwritten date: Galtellì, December 28th 1897. And a cipher on the back: AQB and the number 28.

Now there was no doubt about it. Say what you like, Bustianu had been right. Anything plainer than that! The cipher, whatever its meaning, showed that the photographs, the branding and the young man's portrait, had been taken one after the other. On the 28th of December. The same day as the disappearance of the lambs. So Zenobi was innocent.

Then Bustianu got moving, though he still didn't understand what motive Zenobi might have had for eliminating the photographer, and along with him all the proofs of his innocence.

* * *

When you come to think of it, it's like writing a poem: the right words come to you without your knowing how. The lines arrange themselves, against all logic, despite all the odds. I've never been a positivist! Never a slave to anything, not even to Reason at all costs. Still less to physiognomy. But even if I had been ... it would have been useful to me now, because if we admit that there is such a thing as a guilty face, it means there is also such a thing as an innocent one. And Zenobi was innocence personified. This wasn't the reason why I dug my heels in, nor was it for his looks, nor for the tenderness in the eyes of Sisinnia, and even less for any belief on my part in the so-called Robin Hood myth.

It was a question of feeling things and assigning them to the only possible place allotted to them. As I said, just like writing a poem.

I have never been a Manichee, never one of those who think they have the truth in their pocket. But I'm ready and willing to fight for what I feel is the truth.

My mother Raimonda taught me that. And then she regretted it, blamed herself for having brought up a son in her own image and likeness. "Sooner or later we'll both come to a bad end," she predicted. Because she well knew, we both knew, that when two people know each other as we knew each other the battles become long and extenuating. And they are made up of predictable actions, moves foreseen in advance. They are the result of a strategy worn threadbare. Never anything else. Keeping mum when you ought to speak, speaking when you'd do better to hold your tongue. Always the same old thing.

As a child I retreated into a stubborn silence. I was touchy, testy, quick to take offence. This my mother knew. She therefore said nothing either, she confined herself to looking at me. And that I knew. So I prepared myself for the battle of silences, with many a thought in my head.

Away from home it was quite another matter: I was practically a chatterbox. And like everyone who is too self-controlled, I went rather too far. My voice too loud, my laughter too hearty, my scrutiny too penetrating.

But there was also my body, a bulky, imposing body. Taller than most. A broad, hairy face. Nothing noble about it. Flesh kneaded of rye and bran.

A rough diamond, a civilized barbarian, an unpolished gentleman.

All things that come in handy in the law courts. Especially in our part of the world. Things that subdue a rowdy public, that make bored judges smile, that cause even embalmed Clerks of the Court to raise their heads. Things that light a spark of interest in the lifeless eyes of the lawyerish caste.

With no opportunities to become an actor, I became

a lawyer. Which means dressing the part. Which calls for studied intonation and sweeping gestures.

The man was a different thing and often in conflict with the orator. He was smaller than his physique suggested, he was prey to doubt.

The man was another thing. He was a child. A child fearful and in awe of others. A taciturn child. An obstinate child.

6

SERGEANT POLI PUFFED WARM BREATH ON THE
fingers of his right hand.

"You mean you went up into the hills even on a cold
day like this?" he asked.

Bustianu nodded. "It's a habit. My legs go of their
own accord. And anyway, walking warms one up."

"So does a good fire and a blanket," teased the sergeant.

"Well, what do you have to tell me?" asked Bustianu
on a note of urgency.

"I've done what you asked me to, even though I don't
understand what you're getting at. And . . ."

"And . . . ?"

"And I've had an answer from the police station in
Orosei. You are perfectly correct: that photographer
Leccis travelled the length and breadth of the Baronìa
from the 20th to the 28th of December of last year. All
his permits in order."

With the hint of a smile Bustianu drew the two photographs from the pocket of his greatcoat. He laid them on the desk right under the sergeant's nose.

Arturo Poli scanned them for a very long time indeed. Not having his pince-nez handy, he half-closed his eyes to focus them better. Then he raised his eyes to meet Bustianu's.

"Zenobi Sanna," said the latter, pointing to the photograph which he himself had dubbed "Portrait of a Young Man". The sergeant said nothing. "Zenobi Sanna and Luigi Piredda busy branding cattle for Cosma Casùla Pes," he continued, indicating the other photograph. "With a date," he added.

The sergeant laughed out loud. "I still don't follow you," he declared, but it was obviously not true.

"I can help you there. If Zenobi Sanna was at Galtellì on the 28th of December, he cannot have been at Marreri that same night to steal his employer's sheep. Secondly, seeing that he had had himself photographed he had no reason to eliminate the photographer. In a word, he is extraneous to the facts attributed to him."

"Do you mean that the murder of Leccis is not connected to the Casùla Pes affair?"

"I mean nothing of the sort. I only said that it was not Zenobi Sanna who killed him. The matter is much simpler than it appears to be. Cosma Casùla Pes does not want Zenobi for a son-in-law. He has an only daughter, Sisinnia. He would jump in the lake rather than deny her wishes. He therefore organizes the business with the lambs. He sends Zenobi to Galtellì and arranges for Luigi Piredda to keep him there for at least forty-eight hours. He has no way of knowing about the photographer, and Piredda can only warn him when it is too late. In the meanwhile a simple question of indemnifying Casùla Pes is complicated by the fact that the young man will not give in. He declares that he is innocent and unjustly accused. He takes to the bush to avoid arrest. Casùla Pes gets scared, he is afraid of retaliations. All the more so because his man down at Galtellì, Luigi Piredda, has informed him about the photographs. It therefore becomes indispensable to eliminate the photographer, and with him everything that might prove that Zenobi Sanna was at Galtellì for the branding. He employs Piredda himself for this purpose. In exchange he provides him with enough money to emigrate to America. But his luck is against him, because the photographs, fresh from the darkroom, have already been delivered. One to Galtellì, the other to Nùoro. And here they are."

"All right, but in the meantime Cosma Casùla Pes is murdered, and Sanna, although the victim of an injustice – something which needs further investigation, you understand – is still the leading suspect. So we are back at square one."

This, however, is what the sergeant said, whereas Bustianu thought exactly the opposite. Things weren't as cut and dried as all that! It is all too easy to send men to gaol. Especially the poor. If anything, the starting point was that Zenobi ought to be exonerated on all charges and publicly rehabilitated. As to the death of Cosma Casùla Pes, it had to be properly investigated. With any luck something might emerge.

When they bury Don Cosma the whole town is there. Donna Dolores seems like the Madonna of the Seven Sorrows, for it takes three people to support her as she follows the coffin. Then comes Sisinnia, upright as a spindle, with her black kerchief pulled so low over her brow that the shadow of it hides her face right down to her chin. There is Bartolomeo Casùla Pes, the brother, brother-in-law and uncle respectively of those concerned. He is thirtyish, thinner and taller than his dead brother. He follows the bier with bared head, his thinning hair exposed to all eyes. A bluish tinge in his gaunt face, but pallor on his ample brow. His eyebrows are two crow's wings and his eyes are steel-blue embers. A handsome race, the Casùla Pes, a well-set-up family. But an unlucky one as well, having no male heirs. For after Sisinnia, Donna Dolores was unable to bear more children, and as for Bartolomeo marrying, there was no question of it. More of a priest

62

than anything else, more in church than on the farm. But money sense, that he had. The ready-reckoner of the family firm.

Then come the rest: relatives to the fourth remove, neighbours, proprietors of adjacent lands, farmhands, the local authorities. A swarm of people there for the funeral. The pomp, the display typical of this part of the world: the little orphan girls dressed in white like angels, the novices in their grey nun's habits, the prior of San Francesco with his entire retinue.

Before the procession the house is a place of lamentation. Sorrow heaped on sorrow. By the hired mourners and the despair of the relatives. It is a place of remembrance, of his wondrous life, of his good looks, his honesty, his perfection. Which seems all the more perfect the more certain it is that the person they are talking about is dead. More than a hero. More than a saint. A corpse. A corpse to praise, to carry in procession, to expose to view. A corpse to be implored: Awake! rise again, breathe again! A corpse to scorn for having yielded to death. One to be mourned here and now, so that not a second may pass without the horror of his absence.

Domo rutta! Sepulta domus! Crumbling walls. Life collapsing upon a faithful wife and a daughter of marriageable age. On a brother defenceless and weak, half man, half priest.

"You've made me do this into the bargain," said Sergeant Poli, with simulated grumpiness. Bustianu took a seat with a half-smile on his face. "It was embarrassing," concluded the sergeant.

"But necessary," said Bustianu. "So what does Bartolomeo have to say?"

"Nothing. Nothing at all. His usual self, for goodness' sake, as polite as could be. Even too polite, if I may say so. He made no comment when I showed up. At my service, in fact. He can find nothing: no sum paid to Piredda, no pay-off on leaving their service. No sign even that he has gone to America. But according to him these matters were entirely in his late brother's hands, God rest him. Not to mention the fact that the farm at Galtellì belonged to his sister-in-law."

"What, to Donna Dolores?"

"Precisely. And therefore outside his financial control."

"Therefore the farm at Galtellì was not part of the estate itself?"

"It seems not. In fact it appears that Donna Dolores dealt with it personally."

"How interesting," commented Bustianu.

"Even though I am inclined not to believe this. I mean to say, a woman looking after such matters!"

continued Sergeant Poli.

"Ah, Sergeant, it's quite clear that you don't know the women of these parts!"

7

TONGUES WAGGED, JUST FOR THE SAKE OF WAGGING of course, because most people don't realize what they are saying when they open their mouths. Let alone in those days, when there was little in the way of distractions. So what did they do? They talked of this and that. And gossip worked perfectly well even before the telephone. For example, someone might come up with a spot of guesswork, such as that the woman had a lover, and not only that but was also pregnant.

It must be said that, frankly, if people talked they had something to talk about. In this case, moreover, it was so obvious that there was something fishy about the death of Cosma Casùla Pes that scarcely a word was spoken. Glances were exchanged, eyebrows were raised and that said everything. For example, that this business of the murder had fallen pat, right on cue, just as Bartolomeo Casùla Pes's thirtieth birthday was coming up. For according to his father's will, if he reached thirty years of age without issue he could lay a claim only to such an annual income as would enable him to live in a dignified mànner but not enough to play the *grand seigneur*. It made one think . . . it looked not quite right, not something to pass unnoticed. Even if it seemed impossible that this saintly Bartolomeo, with nothing on his mind except his studies and the parish . . . a man who did not womanize, who seemed to be so aloof and all. However, when it came to money he knew what was what, by heaven he did! There were no two ways about it, he was just like his father Battista, who had bought Sa Serra for a song in 1868. And he'd hung on to the property even after the riots of the 26th of April. Cosma had been an entirely different sort of person, unpolished perhaps and pretty much uncultured, a real son of the soil, a good man who always kept his word. When he died everyone was genuinely sorry.

Not to speak of Donna Dolores, who played the lady and the *grande dame* and appeared to be the mistress and matriarch of all. But no use asking her the simplest question, it was always Bartolomeo who came up with the answer. Good lord, how they understood each other, those two, they stuck to money like leeches. They say that in the matter of the will of Battista Casùla Pes she was quite angry with her brother-in-law because he was against claiming rent for a farm at Convento which had remained in the hands of the Dean and Chapter even after the abrogation of the law of mortmain. Because he was hand in glove with the priests, and had no wish to lay claim to a farm which had always been in their hands. But she was dead against this, there was no way of appeasing her.

My father spoke of it as a famous story. He said that on leaving church after the Novena at the Madonna delle Grazie Donna Dolores had turned to her brother-in-law and told him that if he didn't hurry up and have a family what he should be worrying about was where his next meal was coming from, rather than raising questions about the estate. My father said Bartolomeo went as white as a sheet but made no reply. But Cosma had turned round with a laugh and said that there were still two years to run, and that the farm could perfectly well wait, since there were no prospective buyers anyway. No business in prospect, in short, so they could go on leaving it in the hands of the priests. He had then said that in two years anything could happen, he himself might even pass on, never mind reaching thirty, in which case, family or no family, everything would go to Bartolomeo, seeing that he himself had no male heirs. And thereupon, my father told me, Donna Dolores crossed herself and said "God forbid!" And he went on to tell me that it wasn't a matter of buyers, business or any such thing, but it seemed ridiculous to Donna Dolores that after all they had spent to redeem the place they shouldn't enjoy the income from it. Because Bartolomeo refused to ask the priests for even a peppercorn rent.

* * *

I had so many things buzzing through my head! So many that I had a hard time putting them in order. The same thing sometimes happened to me in my study. If I didn't tidy a file away at once it ended with my not being able to lay my hands on it. So my mother told me you must put things in order as you go along, when they are still manageable. For if you once let things get into a muddle it discourages you, and you can't keep things together, and waste a lot of time. While, on the other hand, if you set aside the few moments you need to put a thing in its right place at once, after that it's so much time gained, because everything is there when you want it.

* * *

Raimonda gave her son a straight look. "What d'you expect me to know about such things? I'm not one to listen to tittle-tattle."

Bustianu left off scrutinizing the lamb and fennel stew that lay on his plate. "But how do you see it? Are Dolores and Bartolomeo on friendly terms or not?"

Raimonda shrugged. "As far as I know they're on the best of terms."

69

"Then what about the estate there at the Convento?"

"There's talk about it, but no need to believe it, because they bought that land and assigned it to the priests rent-free, as Bartolomeo wished."

"Yes, but they say he didn't even want to buy it in the first place."

"You know what I say? This is all rubbish. Buying it wasn't a problem for them. Only that he wanted to buy it to leave it to the priests. It was she who had no intention of leaving it to the priests without earning a penny from it! That's the fact of the matter. Nothing to do with buying or not buying."

"What about Cosma?"

"Oh he, God rest his soul, did what he was told to do by his wife, once she'd talked it over with her brother-in-law."

"Therefore it is possible that Cosma was not even opposed to a marriage between Sisinnia and Zenobi Sanna."

Raimonda came and sat down in a chair immediately facing him. "Bustià," she said calmly, "just drop it, will you? That boy has cooked his own goose. He should have listened to those who knew what's what. At this point, what difference does it make whether he's guilty or not!"

"It makes all the difference, believe you me!" Bustianu's voice had risen by about two octaves.

"Don't yell at me!" yelled Raimonda. "I've told you what I think, but you go ahead and do as you wish. Go on wasting time over these things! And eat up what you've got on your plate!"

But he didn't give up. He couldn't. He was unable to lie down under it and say have it your own way, hunt down that youngster, put a price on his head and add him to the notebooks of the coppers' narks and there's an end to it. The fact was that no-one cared about knowing the truth. It was easier that way, it didn't tread on the toes of important people. It was hard to ask for explanations from folks like the Casùla Pes, and they certainly weren't offering any. What they did they did, and that was that. If they made a decision they made it, and that was that. Neither the police nor the law carried any weight with them.

* * *

No, I didn't give up. It was out of the question. There was evidence enough to investigate them up to the hilt. But it seemed that no-one else cared. As in the worst tradition, once an alleged culprit had been picked on, they went ahead as if the word "alleged" did not exist.

I asked myself a host of questions. Where was Bartolomeo when his brother was murdered? Was Donna Dolores in league with her brother-in-law? Nothing out of the way if they'd settled the matter of the will between themselves. I would not be surprised to discover that they'd even organized the trick with the lambs. Where was Donna Dolores when her husband was killed? Who gave Luigi Piredda his fare to America and paid him off on leaving their employment?

Here, I said to myself, is the contrary side to the fugitive from justice. Here is the result of cut-and-dried solutions. Because, not to put too fine a point on it, the questions I've raised would have been normal, quite routine, anywhere else. But here we have outlaws, I told myself. Both real and "alleged".

Cosma Casùla Pes could have been killed by at least three people.

First, the brother, whose movements on the day of the murder were unknown, though on the other hand no-one had asked him about them.

Then Donna Dolores, yes, gentlemen, the woman herself. She could have had her motives. She had a loving husband, but too submissive, not very enterprising or given to decision, to making money. It wouldn't have surprised me if it transpired that she herself had shot her husband. In both cases it would explain why Cosma had allowed his murderer to take his gun without arousing his suspicion. Cosma was not asleep when he was killed! I could bet my life that he was not asleep. He was awake and on his feet. He perfectly well saw who killed him, who had taken his gun from where it leant against the olive tree. But he did nothing. Nothing at all. Why not? Because he knew his murderer.

But I said three persons. Bartolomeo, all very well. Donna Dolores, very well too. But there was also Luigi Piredda. Who could lay hands on him? Who knew where he was, even? In America . . . Maybe his task had been this very one, the task for which he had been paid, you understand.

There was even the possibility that the murder of Cosma Casùla Pes had no connection with the attachment between Sisinnia and Zenobi.

Things had panned out in such a way that everyone was perfectly content. Except Zenobi, except Sisinnia, except Tzia Rosina.

Except me.

73

8

THE FAREWELL BANQUET FOR HIS MAJESTY'S ROYAL Prosecutor did not get off to a good start. The wife of the mayor of Olíena was taken ill. Corseted up in "mainland" style, put to the torture for the sake of restraining the exuberance of her hips, she had fainted only moments after entering the room on her husband's arm. The journey was to blame, perhaps. The constant series of bends that the carriage had assailed with as much haste as caution in bearing them to Nùoro on that cold evening of January the 16th 1898. There followed the inevitable confusion: ladies who had infallible advice to offer, doctors (in order of seniority) who felt her pulse, servants who rushed about damping napkins to bathe her forehead.

Bustianu was content to observe all this from the sidelines. He had found himself a snug little armchair against the wall of the dining room where, with frantic precision, they were laying the tables for the banquet. They had brought in waiters in livery, a famous chef, and a soprano from Cagliari. The orchestra, scarcely more than a string quartet, had taken its place in the adjacent drawing room, where there would be dancing, and was miaowing away at the latest Viennese waltzes.

Everyone was there. The leading notaries, Salvatore Maccioni and the Nobile Salvatore Satta Carroni. What this title of nobility derived from was anybody's guess. Someone so minded could make a novel out of it . . .

There was the entire Nùoro legal establishment present: Luigi Are, Salvatore Satta Marchi, Giuseppe Pinna, and naturally, as host of the evening, Avvocato Francesco Mastino.

There was Ingegnere Luigi Mura. And the Dean of the Chapter, Don Podda. And the Collaris, the Piratis, the Siottos, the Galisais . . .

Then came the most prominent local landowners, distinguished by their smart country dress, since they had not abandoned the traditional Sardinian costume.

They were followed by the mayors of Orgòsolo, Bitti, Mamoiada and Nùoro, and the mayor of Olíena of whom we have already spoken because of his wife's malaise.

There also was Sergeant Poli, in high dress uniform, amongst the representatives of the forces of law and order and of the High Command at Cagliari.

His Majesty's Royal Prosecutor and his consort arrived with perfect punctuality, twenty minutes late.

Here and there, in the ample apartments prepared for the reception, and lit by the most up-to-date lighting, it was all a whirl of veils, ostrich feathers and even fans. Dresses *à la dernière mode parisienne* were forcing flabby figures into shape, and blossoming into fashionable puffed sleeves and revealing décolletés.

"So you're here," said Sergeant Poli, offering Bustianu a glass of bubbly yellowish liquid.

"Uh-huh," replied he, seeing no point in answering what was already obvious.

"You don't seem to be enjoying yourself very much," continued the sergeant.

"I am not enjoying myself at all," confirmed Bustianu.

"Everyone is seeking you out, especially the ladies. I think they want you to read them something, particularly some of your own poems."

"In which case I would prefer them not to find me. I'll take to the hills. Tell them you haven't found me."

"I simply can't", bridled the sergeant. "The mistress of the house would never forgive me. And then, I've sworn the oath never to lie."

"In that case tell them you found me, but couldn't catch me."

"Then they'll force me to put out a search for you, maybe to put a price on your head . . ."

It was at this point that the mistress of the house came sailing in: "Look here, this evening I won't take no for an answer. Don't hold out on me, Bustià, you must read us some little thing. But you musn't go scaring our guests with things like the *Rebel Verses*, read us one of those things full of tender feeling that you do so well . . . "

"Not this evening", broke in Bustianu. His tone of voice was not in the least brusque, yet it bore no rebuttal. "I don't wish to spoil your party," he added, taking his hostess gently by the arm. "Your husband would never speak to me again. This is good wine . . . " he pursued inconsequentially. "When is the singer coming on? My goodness, all the way from Cagliari! I can scarcely wait to hear her . . . "

A slight smile hovered on Sergeant Poli's lips as he observed Bustianu, with Signora Mastino not daring to say a word, making for the ballroom.

"The identity of a people!" His Majesty's Prosecutor was remarking, before he took a bite out of a boiled potato. "The identity of this people of Sardinia, so hard-working, so honest in its rustic sobriety, but – allow me to say – so very touchy. There is no nook or cranny around this part of the world where this word 'identity' isn't dragged in to justify every sort of abuse. Some rascal commits an act of theft? Identity. A young man rebels against law and order? Identity again . . . " There followed a silence which but for the clattering of cutlery would have been embarrassing. "I have never been inclined to tolerate such propensities," persisted the Prosecutor. "After all, a nation is a nation. Certain sacrifices simply have to be made! Progress and modernity exact a price that has to be paid. And permit me to say . . . " he added, turning towards Bustianu, "permit me to say that we are often obliged to rectify customs that can only be termed flagrantly medieval, to put it mildly, though I should sooner call them downright primitive."

Bustianu stared for a second or two at the boiled potatoes surrounding his fillet of beef *au poivre*. He pronged one with a fork as if it were the most important decision he had made in his life. "Primitive," he said, laying down his fork on the side of his plate. "So primitive that many really modern anthropological studies have it that such customs are an example of social living that still holds good."

"These are mere flippancies," retorted the Prosecutor. "You are alluding to purely academic discussions, not to the administration of a whole nation!"

"I am referring to the free use of the common lands, which now, thanks to your modernity, is forbidden. I am referring to the modernity that has created vast enclosed estates where previously they did not exist,

78

Your Excellency. Maybe we were primitive, but as for the Middle Ages, you brought them to our island with you!"

"Middle Ages, Middle Ages, what's all that terrible about the Middle Ages?" asked Canon Podda, addressing the wife of the mayor of Bitti, who was seated beside him.

"It's all these Socialist notions: everything belongs to everyone. So no-one accepts their own responsibilities." The Prosecutor's voice had taken on a somewhat more acid note. "But your insular identity is safe. Isn't that what matters to you?"

"If I may put in a word, that is not what he meant," intervened our host. "Bustianu has a brusque way with him, but he's not altogether wrong. How to build a new nation is something we should all discuss together. What works for the Sicilians doesn't necessarily work for us Sardinians, you understand."

"Even on this question of identity we don't see eye to eye, Your Excellency," explained Bustianu. "It may surprise you to know that a fixed identity, an idea you seem to attribute to me, is in my view an aberration. I believe in a provisional identity, one in a state of flux, that finds in itself the mechanisms to prevent its being erased altogether . . . "

"Even if this encourages those who prefer an eye for an eye and a tooth for a tooth, atavistic customs,

79

rather than the law of the land, which is equal for all!" The Prosecutor's sarcasm was becoming quite immoderate.

"There is no question but that we are having a lot of trouble introducing laws that are often incomprehensible to the people in these parts," rumbled the mayor of Bitti, clearing his throat.

"I can see what you're after," grumbled the Prosecutor. "You won't take the rough with the smooth. You want the benefits without the sacrifices entailed."

"What we want is to make our contribution," put in Bustianu.

"Do we really have to go on talking about things quite so tedious as these?" broke in the lady of the house. "We are here to celebrate, and as usual you all bore us to death with these impossible disputes. I propose a toast," said she, raising her glass . . .

"True to form, you can't manage to hold your tongue, Bustià," said our host Francesco Mastino, shaking his head reproachfully. They were seated off to one side with steaming cups of coffee before them.

On the opposite side of the room the Prosecutor was telling amusing anecdotes to an all-male audience wreathed in dense clouds of tobacco smoke. "My wife wanted to try her hand too," he was saying. "So she picked up the gun and fired it. The recoil knocked her

backwards like a straw in the wind. Ah, women! . . ."
he added, and some even laughed.

Bustianu leapt to his feet, looked for somewhere to put
down his coffee cup: "I have to speak to Sergeant Poli!"

Francesco Mastino gave him a puzzled look.

"That's it, that's it! I should have thought of it sooner,
dammit! I have to have a word with the sergeant!"
continued Bustianu without paying him the least attention.

"Still the same old story!" exclaimed Francesco
Mastino, receiving a hard stare from Bustianu in return.

* * *

Mastino declared that I was being childish. He declared
that this whole business had become a fixation with
me. And he was right enough. All the same, I think he
was the first to understand me. Because he knew how
far I was prepared to go to make doubt prevail over
certainty. It had frequently been the case with himself
as well. I reminded him of the fact that he, against all
odds, had achieved the acquittal of that shepherd from
Ovodda implicated in the kidnapping of Dr —. That
he had refused to give up. That he had carried on despite
everything.

Now it was clear, as clear as daylight. How on earth
could I have missed it? The shot! It was the work of the
woman herself! That explained everything.

At that moment I would have been wide open to any rebuke whatever. I would even have been able to put up with sarcasm. The sarcasm of whoever wished to say that hidden under the apparent cool of my ashes there were still glowing embers. And maybe he would have been able to put a name to those embers: Zanobi Sanna.

Very well, very well, I am the first to admit it. Months passed, and things seemed to have taken their predestined course. But I wasn't giving up. And if they thought that in this outlying region of the Kingdom of Italy a summary judgment was enough, any sort of decision whatever, well, they were wrong.

It may be that we're too stubborn here in our part of the world, too set in our ways, too reluctant to yield to change. But not stupid. Not in the least.

And a whole lot less uncivilized than they thought us!

* * *

Meanwhile tongues were wagging. They wagged mightily. The more time passed the higher rose the price on Zenobi's head. He was seen everywhere. If you believed all the rumours he was a member of every gang of bandits, even the worst of them. On occasions he had been sighted in two different places at once. Like Billy the Kid. The pretty boy of Nùoro, the legendary brigand, angelic to look at and pitiless at heart. He'd been seen on his horse near Cuglieri only a few hours after being sighted in the vicinity of Orune – miles away. They said he was hand-in-glove with the brigand Derosas, and much more besides. They said that with his infallible aim he had done to death at least ten people without even being seen. So infallible an aim he had that even Corbeddu of Olíena took off his cap at the mere mention of his name.

Not to speak of his amatory exploits. If you were to ask them, ten women out of ten were ready to die for him.

A legend. The worst disease there is. Ball and chain for a young man whose only wish was to take to himself a wife, and to live his own life.

"They wanted to do things beyond their power, that's the fact of the matter. With that mother of his who has always treated him like a little prince, whereas they're just common folk. Plain, decent folk, but no more," said Raimonda as she damped down the washing before ironing it.

February was there outside the windows and the afternoons were getting warmer.

Bustianu looked up from the book he was reading. He glanced at his mother and curled his upper lip. "No caste, no justice," he replied, closing his book and putting a finger in to mark his place.

Raimonda heaved a long, long sigh. She dared not

83

look at him. She seemed to be absorbed in some thought many miles away. "You want to change the world," she said at last. "But in the end it'll be the world that changes you. Things are as they are."

"In that case one can spare oneself the effort of living in this world," retorted Bustianu, as he went back to his book. There followed some minutes of silence, broken only by the relentless ticking of the grandfather clock out in the hall.

"I sometimes wonder," said Raimonda after a while, "what sort of a head you have on your shoulders. It's all very well to do your level best by a client who collaborates with you, but this Zenobi Sanna, it seems to me he doesn't even want to be defended! Look, he doesn't even bother to see you, and that's a fact!"

"I am convinced that's not how things went. I'm sure that no-one wants to investigate this business. And if this is what I think, just imagine what *he* thinks! This is why he doesn't turn himself in. If at least he had some guarantee, some safeguard . . . "

"Guarantees, guarantees, you sound like your father. Going on like this one can only end up in trouble. D'you think people don't talk? Don't you think that word hasn't gone round as to what's going on? It's a question of money! A lot of money! And then if you add to that property, land, livestock, then you'll get the picture. D'you follow me?"

"It was Donna Dolores . . . "

" . . . In the name of your dear father, God rest his soul, I refuse to listen to this kind of talk."

"It was her! There's no other explanation. She followed him to Marreri and she shot him. That's why he put up no resistance."

"Stop. That's enough. I'll not hear another word."

9

MY FATHER TELLS ME THAT TZIA ROSINA KEPT
on and on until she had persuaded her son to talk to
Bustianu. She had tried everything, poor woman, but
eventually she blackmailed him by saying that if he didn't
agree she'd curse him from her grave, because that's
where he was bringing her by his stubbornness. And her
son, disfigured by months on the run, embittered by the
thought of being a hunted animal, aged by the atrocious
life he lived as a fugitive, had asked his mother for a hot
meal and said, all right, he would meet this lawyer she
was going on about, even if he was by no means sure that
any lawyer could be a trustworthy person.

As for the mother, she swore till she was blue in the
face, by the Good Lord and every saint in heaven that
if he was ever stabbed in the back it would be none of
her doing, who in Heaven's name did he take her for?
Someone who would betray her own kith and kin?

And she wept in silence, as only mothers can weep over their own children.

Very well, said Zenobi – to stop her tormenting him about this lawyer! Things could not get any worse, with a charge of murder on his head.

So Tzia Rosina warmed up the soup, made a tub of hot water for him to wash in, ironed him clean shirts and underwear, and last thing, before seeing him off, asked him when. Zenobi, standing in the doorway to the kitchen garden, a couple of hours before dawn, said, "I'll let you know." And she, giving him a great hug, said, "You've promised." And he, shouldering his bag of crisp carasau bread and pear-shaped cheeses, said: "I will do it for you."

They found themselves face to face. Bustianu ran into him right outside his house. It was nearly ten o'clock at night. The sky was pitch black, no moon.

"Let's go somewhere safer," said Zenobi, leading the way.

Bustianu didn't stir a limb. He could scarcely see him in the darkness. "My own house is a safe place," he said. "Since you've taken the trouble to make your way right up to the door."

"You're not alone," said Zenobi.

Bustianu took his watch from his waistcoat pocket. "At this hour of night," he said, "it's as if I were alone.

My mother sleeps on the other side of the house, and our maid doesn't live in. Let's go to my study. No-one will think of looking for us there."

Zenobi eyed him for a moment or two, then he smiled. His fair hair, his eyes, his teeth, gleamed through the darkness. "Forgive my distrust," said he, hoisting his gun back onto his shoulder. "I'm doing this for my mother's sake," he added, moving towards the house.

When he entered the lawyer's study he gave a quick glance around as if expecting an ambush.

"You run no risk here," repeated Bustianu as he lit the lamp on the table.

Zenobi propped his gun in a corner piled high with legal files and remained on his feet before the desk.

"Take a seat," said Bustianu, pointing to a chair opposite him. Then he started rummaging behind the door of a little cupboard down beside him. Zenobi gave a quick glance at his gun, within arm's reach. "I must have something to drink around here," said Bustianu. "Oh, here it is: Vernaccia," he added, holding up the bottle before raising himself above the level of the desk.

Zenobi seemed to relax. "I don't trust anyone nowa-days," he apologized with another smile. And Bustianu realized the force of that smile, of the harmony of features that were perfection itself. He found himself thinking how much the features of people who love one another also come to resemble each other, and scrutinized Zenobi's face for the perfection of Sisinnia's. "If you want to get out of this situation," he said, "You simply have to trust someone."

The young man shook his head. "What's done is done, Avvocato! There's nothing left to hope for."

"Nonsense, there's plenty to hope for! To start with, the charge of your stealing the lambs doesn't stand up."

"Oh, that . . . " commented Zenobi with a shrug.

"Don't underestimate things. That's really important. You've been sentenced for a crime you didn't commit. There's a photograph to prove it."

Zenobi finally sat down. "Didn't he take it away with him?" he asked.

"No, Luigi Piredda left it in the hands of his mother before he went off, or maybe it was delivered directly to her when he had already left. What matters is that it is now in our own hands."

"So they killed the photographer for nothing."

"Nothing at all. But there's a date on that photograph, December the 28th. I'd like to be sure that it's the correct date."

"That's the date all right. But you see they can say that a date can always be added afterwards."

"Yes, they could say that, I've already thought of it. But there's also a serial number."

"I know, but they can also say that I wrote it myself,

because the fire in his studio destroyed everything."

"I've thought of that too, but what they can't deny is that the photograph was taken at Galtellì."

Zenobi attempted another smile. "So what?" he asked. "I went down to Galtellì at least once a month." And after a moment he added: "You see there's nothing to hang on to, nothing at all."

"Sergeant Poli doesn't see it that way. But . . . "

" . . . But he's tied hand and foot, Avvocato. He's like a two of clubs when diamonds are trumps."

Bustianu was forced to admit that Zenobi was right on that score. "Yes, but we mustn't let that put us off. It mustn't distract us."

"We all have our hands tied, Avvocato," remarked Zenobi, bitterly. "If only I were able to say what I know . . . "

"To me you can say it. Chances are we'll sort the matter out."

Zenobi slumped back in his chair, shutting his eyes as if to chase away an unwelcome picture. "There are people whom I don't want to implicate, in fact I can't."

"Sisinnia?"

Zenobi gave an imperceptible nod. "She mustn't be brought into this business. I'd rather give myself up, I'd rather let them kill me."

"Let's try and talk about the afternoon when Cosma Casùla Pes was murdered."

Zenobi raised a hand and rubbed the back of his neck. "I was there," he said in all simplicity.

Bustianu lunged forward so suddenly that his chest thumped on the desktop. "You were there?" he gasped, with the bottle of Vernaccia still clasped in his fist.

"At Marreri, to see Sisinnia," explained Zenobi. "We heard the shot and thought that Cosma had bagged a hare or a partridge. And then . . . "

"And then?" urged Bustianu, putting down the bottle on the desk.

"Sisinnia suddenly got scared, and we ran up to the old olive tree and saw what there was to see."

"What did you see, Zenobi?"

"I can't," was all he could say. "You know as well as I do that I can't say a word."

"Donna Dolores?" demanded Bustianu, and his lip was trembling.

Zenobi went on shaking his head slowly.

"Trust me! If anything is to be done for you and Sisinnia, then be candid with me!"

"*Sos meres* . . . Her people." Thus Zenobi surrendered.

"Bartolomeo?" insisted Bustianu.

"Bartolomeo and Donna Dolores," confirmed Zenobi. "It's a family matter, Avvocato. It's a thing to be sorted out within the family. Cosma had ideas all of his own. He was angry at his brother. There were constant arguments over a certain piece of land . . . "

"The Convento farm?"

"Just that. Cosma wanted to give it to Sisinnia as a dowry, and Bartolomeo wouldn't have it."

"And Donna Dolores?"

"Oh, she never says a word. She acts. You can never guess what's in her mind. Try asking her where she was that afternoon! Those two made a pact, Avvocato, and the result is that I'm a dead man."

"So they made a pact. But why? What possible interest could Donna Dolores have in getting her husband killed? Or else . . . in killing him herself?"

"She'd have been up to it." Zenobi laughed. "Take it from me!"

"So that's how things went, in your opinion?"

"I don't know, and I won't speak of what I don't know. All I know is that they were both there that afternoon. And that Donna Dolores had given her brother-in-law a hint. I don't know if I've made myself clear."

"Clear as daylight. I only wonder why you didn't tell me earlier."

"You know why. If anyone is going to destroy Sisinnia's family it won't be me. I'd rather go to gaol. Sisinnia didn't see anything, she was behind me, running as fast as she could."

"If that's the way things went we'll soon find out."

"What do you mean to do?"

"I want to lure the beast out of its lair, and to do so I

have to delve into the lair, you understand?"

"You mean Donna Dolores?

"The very one. I shall deal with Don Bartolomeo. You'll see that if a certain idea of mine comes off he will break cover. Incidentally, are you hungry? If you come to the kitchen there may be some leftovers."

"No, thank you, I'm not hungry. Why are you doing this?"

"What?"

"Why are you doing all this? What have you got to gain from it?"

"Nothing. It's my job."

He had a very crafty plan, for he was a real old fox, was Bustianu. His idea was that if he could break the links of common interest between Bartolomeo and Donna Dolores they would tear each other to shreds. Cosma's death solved a lot of problems. The inheritance, for example, that would no longer be at the mercy of that famous clause in the will concerning Bartolomeo's thirtieth birthday. Donna Dolores was smart enough to realize that, however things went, Don Bartolomeo would find a loophole to get out of renouncing his share. But above all she knew that her husband was in any case too weak to hold his own against his brother and split the property in half. She was greed personified. Why share out what she could have whole and entire? So the question boiled down to this: once the term of her widow's mourning was over, could Donna Dolores pass from one brother to the other? In the meantime, though, she had made a few mistakes. The first was to think that Bartolomeo was more easily manipulated than his brother, the late lamented Cosma. The second was to underestimate the bond between Zenobi and Sisinnia. And this was a very grave error, because the attempt to part them had only brought them closer together.

To put it briefly, Bustianu's plan was to lead Donna Dolores and Don Bartolomeo to suspect each other, and thence lure them out into the open.

He therefore did one of those things which, looking back at them, seem like madness, but at the moment seem the only right thing to do. He wrote an anonymous letter, imitating one of the many he had received in the past. It took him the best part of the night to cut out and paste on one letter after another:

> Watch out for that great lady Donna Dolores Casùla Pes, who plays the saint but is really the devil incarnate. Upon my oath she was there at Marreri when Don Cosma died.
>
> A Friend

He read it through. It seemed plausible and it could do no harm. It might cause some confusion, give the police a chance to intervene, make a check-up, interview the woman. To break down her immunity, force her to come up with an alibi. Supposing she had one.

He washed, dressed, put the letter in his pocket, and right early in the morning he went to the police station.

"It's plausible, I have to admit. But it's one thing to make a guess and another thing to prove it. And you know that an anonymous communication doesn't cut much ice." Sergeant Poli had a weary look about him.

"Only a check-up, just to keep your conscience clear, Sergeant. You wouldn't like to find yourself in the position of having to say that you hadn't done everything you ought to have done, would you?" Bustianu leant closer to him, so that he could lower his voice. "The thing is as plain as a pikestaff, Sergeant," he urged. "The recoil, Sergeant! It was her! The recoil pushed her backwards. She had aimed at her husband's chest, but she struck him on the neck, the chin, and in the face. That is why the shot seemed so inaccurate. Sergeant, let me tell you, Zenobi could have killed him by a single shot without going anywhere near him. And he'd have used his own gun, he'd never have gone and got the victim's gun. Everyone knows his own gun like he knows his own dog. Zenobi would never have used a weapon he didn't know. Is that so hard to understand?"

"That's a very serious accusation. We cannot proceed on the basis of an anonymous letter. If I do what you ask me to, I can kiss goodbye to my next posting, they'll pack me off to wherever they think fit until my pension comes up. What's more, I'm not going to be all that long in command of this station. I am only temporary. The station chief is arriving any day now."

"All the more reason to make something out of it. To end on a high note. I don't know, but a job really well done could even earn you a promotion. She had the ways and means, Sergeant. This woman used her steward at Galtellì to eliminate the photographer, after which she put up the money to ship him to America. And all of this behind her husband's back."

"Yes, all right, but the question of the lambs . . . "

"Oh, that was just routine. A woman of that stamp had no problem in persuading her husband that it was the quickest and easiest way to prevent Sisinnia from making a wrong marriage. The woman is greedy for money. She is afraid of letting the property go up in smoke. She is also scared that her brother-in-law might marry in time to take up his due share of the estate."

"Let us admit even that. But where has it got her? The risk that he might marry still exists."

"Of course, but she herself is now a candidate for marriage. She is a most beautiful woman, I shouldn't be surprised if she and Bartolomeo had been lovers for quite a while."

"That seems to me unlikely. Their relationship appears

to be not at all friendly."

"In public not, Sergeant, in public not! But look at things from this point of view. Coming out of church after the Novena of the Madonna delle Grazie, when the place was crowded, does that seem to you the rational time to shout and scream about family legacies?"

"Rational no, not at all. But you know that women very rarely are."

"Not that woman, Sergeant. Her brother-in-law's thirtieth birthday is coming up. He seems to be dangerously under the influence of the Dean and Chapter. It would be nothing strange if there were a marriage in the air set up by the priests. She has to move fast. She needs a scapegoat. Zenobi is perfect for the part. Perfect! He took it on himself when he went into hiding. A unique opportunity. She would have expected him to be convicted, either to prison or at least a fine, and passed off the murder of her husband as an act of vengeance. Zenobi's taking to the hills simply made things easier. Investigation closed. Culprit unmasked."

"It all looks difficult to me, Avvocato. Difficult to prove."

"Not so difficult if we do the right things. These are two colossi with feet of clay. Without some pretext they are untouchable, but it would take a mere nothing to make them collapse. Sergeant, they will accuse each other mutually . . . "

97

"So you saw to providing a pretext," commented Sergeant Poli with a glance at the anonymous letter.

Bustianu spread his arms wide. "If there's nothing to it, there's no harm done."

* * *

It was a question of going a roundabout way at the business. Of moving cautiously. Sergeant Poli would tackle Donna Dolores, request an interview with her, and inform her of the anonymous letter. He would ventilate certain suspicions without making any direct accusations.

Apart from that it was simply a matter of waiting. But also of foreseeing what would happen. If I was right, the priests were worried about losing the Convento estate. If the influence of Donna Dolores over her brother-in-law was such as I thought it to be, the Chapter risked the loss of a considerable source of income. Therefore we had to start with the priests. My part was to deal with the priests and Don Bartolomeo Casùla Pes.

* * *

Bustianu's entry into the church has remained an historic event. Because what he thought of the priests and the Church in general was common knowledge, he had turned his back on God, was anti-clerical to the marrow, this we must admit. An excellent fellow, I say it and will say it again, but when it came to the priests he was like the Devil and Holy Water, if you follow me.

So on the pretext of consulting the baptismal register to resolve some legal problems he presented himself in the Chapter House. As calm as if he were at home in that place redolent of candles and incense. The Dean, Don Podda, was staggered to see him there.

"Wait a while before killing the fatted calf! I am here for bureaucratic reasons," said Bustianu, spreading his hands like a ham actor bowing to his audience.

The Dean shook his head, almost pityingly. "Anything can happen, Avvocato. One can even start with bureaucratic reasons and end up serving at Mass."

Bustianu had to chuckle. "That's true enough," he said. "Sometimes things take a turn we haven't foreseen, who knows?"

"Avvocato, you say that as if it were easier for you to fly," hedged the Dean.

"You are too clever for me, Don Podda," conceded Bustianu. "I can't put anything past you. Anyway, you have more important matters to attend to than keeping an eye on a candidate for hellfire."

"If it is God's decree, Avvocato, neither you nor I can do anything about it. What exactly did you need?" enquired Don Podda, forced to throw his head back to look up at Bustianu, who was almost a foot taller.

"Oh, I'm doing a favour to a friend who has to get

99

together the documents for the purchase of a piece of land . . . You'll understand my reticence, the dealings are particularly confidential. Who'd have thought it . . . That land up for sale . . . "

The Dean gave Bustianu a queer sort of look. "A piece of land?" he queried, more to himself than to Bustianu.

"I've made a promise, don't force me to come out with it," said Bustianu pleadingly. "I can only tell you that the offer is a good one, really good. For that land, what's more . . . But the negotiations are entirely confidential, that is why I accepted the task of preparing the documentation, you understand. It is not my field, I am a criminal lawyer. Anyway, I am telling you nothing you don't already know . . . And if you don't know it, then . . . "

"Then?" The Dean was hanging on his lips.

"No no, let's drop the matter. Don't tell me of all people! And don't look at me like that. I am a discreet person, I only mention it to you because I'm sure you have already been informed . . . "

The Dean started to get nervous. "Of course, of course," he stammered. "I think I have grasped what you are speaking of." But he hadn't grasped a thing. Don Podda began passing his first finger inside his stiff collar as if it had become too tight for him.

"In this way a nasty business will come to a happy ending, that at least. More I will not say. In short, a marriage that will put all to rights, those lands will return to the family, and if they agree on the price they'll get a good round sum for it – this I say between you and me. However, to be equally open with one another, I have heard – and I neither confirm nor deny it – that a very generous emolument comes also to the Chapter, to you, in short. After all, you've looked after that land for so long. Have I made myself clear? And now I beg you not to make me add another word . . . "

The Dean tottered, looked for something to hold on to. He seemed to be short of air. "You are speaking of the Convento land?" he wheezed at last.

Bustianu waited a second or two before, with the slightest raise of his eyebrows, affirming it.

The trap was baited. There remained nothing more than to wait until they fell into it.

* * *

Nor had I long to wait.

I had my lifespace in a bare-bleak clearing that formed a sort of terrace on the eastern side of Badde Manna. At the top of the hill of Sant'Onofrio. Already the early spring sun glittered from the rose-grey rock. I took my seat on my own boulder, a granite seat that the wind had carved out for me. I clasped my hands over the top of my stick, rested my chin on them, and let my gaze go wander. A goshawk was searching the ground for hares or fieldmice. A smudge of low-lying cloud darkened the opalescent clarity of the early afternoon. The green of the valley was rich enough for the earth to burst into a soundless explosion:

> In the silence of the earth
> The great soul rejoices

And green is the soul. A great green soul making its way upwards from its rose-grey granite roots. This indeed is Ballero's palette, the way he painted this land-scape. Now one recognizes the porous smudge of the horizon line, towards the sea, beyond the powder-white heights of the great bluff towering over Olíena. And the ashen haze that hovers over the turquoise sea of the Gulf of Orosei.

Then I heard someone behind me.

It was the panting breath of a young man standing there like a petrified juniper tree, waiting for the flow of my thoughts to make a pause. I looked over my shoulder. He was a stunted youngster, bristling with black hair on his jaw and forearms.

"Tell me," began this faun of the woods when I had turned in my seat to face him. "Are you the Avvocato?"

"Indeed I am," said I.

"A certain person wishes to say a few words to you, if it is not inconvenient for you to follow me." His voice was that of an adolescent, though he was a good twenty years old.

"And who might this person be?" I enquired.

"A person of some note, *s'abbocà*! So will you come?"

It was what I had been waiting a whole week for. I gave the lad a nod. Without a second's hesitation he set off down the hill, not leaving me an instant to get to my feet, leading the way some steps ahead.

When we drew level with the Carabinieri barracks I cast a swift glance around. A sentry was loafing beside the entrance.

With a glance at my guide I approached the sentry. "Is Sergeant Poli in?" I asked him, with a backward look at the young man waiting for me without batting an eyelid.

The sentry said yes he was. "I have to give him a very urgent message: it is the moment to pay that visit . . . Just that. He will understand," I added, seeing the sentry looking at me as if I were mad.

Then I returned to my faun. "What are you worried about?" he asked, evidently amused.

"You never can tell," I answered in the tones of one who knows a thing or two. "It's better to be on the safe side."

We went on a few steps. The young man was chuckling to himself.

"Well, where on earth are we going?" I demanded, with a show of annoyance.

"We are there," said he, making for the Cathedral.

"Very well, we are there, but I don't see the meaning

of it. I want to know who wishes to speak to me and where," I thundered, careful not to express any fear or anxiety, but simply exasperation at all this secrecy.

"You have nothing to fear. It's Canon Podda who sent me to fetch you," piped my guide as he led me to the Seminary. Then he stood aside for me to enter. He remained in the bright light of the doorway almost as if to bar off any means of retreat.

The priest arrived from a door at the side of the broad entrance hall. "Please step this way," he said. The shiny black of his threadbare habit and his sturdy figure gave him all the appearance of an aged seal. "Please forgive the method adopted," purred the priest in honeyed tones, indicating a corridor in semi-darkness so narrow that I couldn't have raised my arms in it. "But the person whom I have to bring you to meet has asked for the utmost secrecy."

"It's one mystery after another," was my comment.

"Oh no, no mystery," simpered the priest. "Just a matter of clearing things up." He had a wistful yet triumphant air, like that of a child who has promised not to tell a secret, but can't keep it in.

At the end of this tunnel was a little arch opening into a small vestibule. Two closed doors, one on the left, one on the right.

"Please be patient for another moment," begged the priest, knocking at the right-hand door. As he entered

he turned towards me for a last time. "One moment," he
repeated. Then he disappeared into the room beyond.

* * *

In the meanwhile Donna Dolores had done her utmost
to avoid seeing Sergeant Poli. She only gave way when
she realized that the sergeant had no intention of leaving,
and while with no hint of a threat and indeed most
regretfully telling the maid that in case of refusal he
would be obliged to require her mistress's presence down
at the police station. And even the maid realized that
that would be embarrassing for everyone concerned. She
went on to say that her mistress was at her wits' end, that
you couldn't even recognize her for the person she
was, after what had happened to her family . . . Then
the sergeant, making sure that this Sardinian lass knew
enough Italian to grasp his meaning, said that he understood, he understood very well, but that when the police
receive information they have to follow it up. So Donna
Dolores issued forth from her room. Lovely as a statue.
Dark as a starless night. Her face gaunt, the look in her
eyes as gaunt as her slender hands . . .

* * *

Surrounded by silence. Total. Absolute. As if I had ended
up way down in the centre of the earth. I looked this
way and that. It was a frightful little hole and I felt I could

scarcely breathe in it. By the time Don Podda put his face through the doorway again, beckoning me to follow him, I had almost made up my mind to leave.

The room into which the priest led me was unexpectedly spacious, though in semi-darkness. Furnished in grand style with massive furniture. A few logs were burning in the fireplace. Don Bartolomeo Casùla Pes was standing silhouetted before this fireplace. Seen at close quarters he appeared even taller and thinner. He wore country clothes. His wine-coloured fustian jacket emitted a purplish sheen. "You must excuse the way in which this has been arranged," he said, with his back still turned towards me. "But my deep mourning compels me to the most absolute discretion. You understand. You are a man of the world." His tone of voice was warm, not a hint of mockery.

"I understand perfectly," was all I said.

"The Canon has been at pains to inform me that you have information that concerns me. Concerns my family, that is . . . " He swiftly picked himself up on that one. He was speaking to the fireplace all this time.

I took a look at the priest. He had dwindled into a mere shrimp of a man. He was attempting to shrink back into an armchair behind me. "The Canon has evidently misunderstood," I ventured.

"None of these legal quibblings, Avvocato, we're here to speak out plain and simple." And at this Bartolomeo

Casùla Pes was obliged to turn and look at me. His face was broad, pale, and clean-shaven. His receding hair had heightened his brow, accentuating the crow's wings of his eyebrows.

"May I sit down?" I asked, without addressing anyone in particular.

Bartolomeo Casùla Pes it was who gave me permission with the merest lowering of his bluish eyelids. "They tell me," he said in an extraordinarily placid tone of voice, "that you have been retained as a lawyer with regard to the sale of a certain estate owned by our family. This surprises me, in view of the fact that the land is not for sale."

Don Podda emitted a grunt of satisfaction.

I also tried to put a smile on my face. "My client is an utterly trustworthy person," I pronounced. "If I have been charged with this business, it is that my client is perfectly clear-sighted. It may be that someone in your family has, at it were, considered other possibilities. We are speaking of an estate that increases in value year by year, the town is growing, developing . . . "

Don Podda gave a start and scrabbled at the arms of the chair in the depths of which he was sunk. Breathing hard, he came and stood between Don Bartolomeo and myself. "Tell him!" he commanded of Bartolomeo almost rudely.

Don Bartolomeo thought for a moment, regarding me with eagle eye. "You can tell your so-called client that the assignment of that estate will not be changed," he said in formal tones, but with a trace of hesitancy.

"Very well," I said abruptly. "I shall refer this to my client. However, it was said to be absolutely cut and dried . . . If you now tell me that you have changed your minds, I cannot but take it into consideration."

"Do so!" cried Don Podda, nodding furiously.

"Would you think it ill-mannered on my part to ask for some explanation of what is clearly a mere inference for which no-one holds you directly responsible?" asked Don Bartolomeo, struggling to snatch the right words out of the air before his face.

"Not ill-mannered at all," I replied. I had decided to adopt brevity and reticence in my answers.

"I presume," he went on, "that it is also useless to ask you who was the direct source . . . "

"You presume rightly," said I. "I can only tell you that we speak of a source not only trustworthy, but above suspicion," I added. And wanting to enjoy his reaction, I took a step forwards.

Don Podda seemed forever about to put in a word, but every time he changed his mind.

Don Bartolomeo Casùla Pes bit his lower lip. Then he began: "Since the death of my brother, things have been happening that force me to intervene. I had no wish to do so, Avvocato, because I know you to be an honest person, someone who would never defend a criminal.

But you know how things go around these parts: rumours that cannot be stilled, people have to take the initiative. Our only wish is to be left in peace, Avvocato, we have a tragic death in the family. An unimaginable loss. Why do you want to complicate matters that are so straightforward? That lad condemned himself with his own hands, because if he hadn't done anything he shouldn't have run away from the law."

Don Podda nodded vigorously.

"It's not as simple as that," I replied, after a few moments of reflection. I wanted to know if that conversation was an offer of conciliation or a stone wall. Then: "There are proofs that Zenobi Sanna was not in Nùoro on the night of December 28th, when he was accused of the theft."

"Proofs?" enquired Bartolomeo, without batting an eyelid.

"A pho–to–graph," I enunciated clearly, as I got to my feet. "A photograph taken by a roving photographer down at Galtellì."

"The same photographer who was done to death?"

"I see you are in possession of the facts."

"Sufficiently so."

"Then you realize that if that particular indictment falls flat, all the rest of it is called in question."

"But what question! Nothing is called in question! That scoundrel has to end his days in gaol. Otherwise . . . "

"Otherwise?"

"We are people of some standing in these parts, AvvocatOOO!" shrieked Don Bartolomeo practically in falsetto. And his hands were shaking.

"Is that a threat?" I asked.

"No threat at all," purred Don Podda in the most conciliating tones he could muster. "It is better to leave things as they stand, that's all he wished to say."

"*I* know what I wish to say," shrieked Don Bartolomeo, turning on him in rage. His eyes had become two slivers. "And the Avvocato knows it too. Dig in the dirt and you get muck on your own hands. Throwing mud at honest folk, well really!" he added, almost to himself.

* * *

"You will understand me," Sergeant Poli was saying to Donna Dolores. "I have duties that are incumbent upon me, however unpleasant they may be. You must see that a communication of this sort, well, I prefer you to be informed about it, you will understand."

Donna Dolores confined herself to a swift glance at the anonymous letter, then replaced it on the table as if it were burning her fingers. "People are too nasty-minded and envious," was all she said, and nothing more.

"All the same," insisted Sergeant Poli, "I am sure that it will not be hard for you to demonstrate the falsehood of this piece of nonsense." Donna Dolores curled a contemptuous lip and replied, "I have nothing to demonstrate, Sergeant."

Sergeant Poli gave a nod of agreement but suggested that keeping silent didn't make things any easier. There was still the question of this anonymous letter which had to be registered in the files, and it could well be that Sanna's lawyer might make use of it to cast doubts on the whole case.

Donna Dolores began to breathe rather heavily. "What sort of doubts?" she almost panted.

"Different possibilities," explained the sergeant. "You know how things go in a court of law . . . "

Donna Dolores replied that there were no doubts, no doubts at all. That afternoon she had never stirred out of the house.

"Very well," smiled Sergeant Poli. "There is no problem, then. When asked, you will reply that you were not at Marreri that afternoon."

"Exactly," confirmed Donna Dolores.

In the room in the Seminary the silence had become intolerable. Don Podda was glaring at Bustianu, who was making no move to leave, but stood precisely where he was, motionless, as if awaiting further developments.

"There's nothing more to be said." Thus Bartolomeo Casùla Pes dismissed him. "You may tell your informants that this time they have missed their mark."

Bustianu didn't budge. "There is something more to be said." His voice in that room was like the whisper of a dying man. "I have to speak to you in private, Don Bartolomeo," he added, switching his gaze to Canon Podda, who was now sweating like a pig and attempting to mop his brow with a snow-white handkerchief.

Bartolomeo Casùla Pes heaved a long sigh, then made an abrupt gesture to the priest. Don Podda got to his feet with some effort, gave Bustianu a look full of angst and rancour, and left the room.

"I come to the point at once. And as a practical man you will excuse my frankness. The life of a man, which has been entrusted to my care, depends upon what I am about to tell you."

Bartolomeo Casùla Pes started pinching his chin vigorously with his right hand.

"I am listening," he said.

"You were seen," continued Bustianu, "seen at Marreri a few minutes after the death of your brother. This information has been held secret by the competent authorities. I now put myself in the wrong by revealing it to you. That is why I asked for an interview with no witnesses present."

Don Bartolomeo's eyelids closed, slowly, slowly. Then he asked: "By whom?"

"It doesn't matter. It's purely a question of when. That

is why I wondered whether, if you had some explanation for your presence at Marreri, you might not prefer to give it to me, even if unofficially, rather than going to the police to make a signed statement."

"And by what authority are you acting, if I may ask?" Don Bartolomeo's voice was getting more tremulous every moment.

"Simply the fact that I am the only person who can help you. And the fact that I do not take you for a murderer."

Bartolomeo Casùla Pes swayed slightly on his feet. Then, "It couldn't go on," he said, "I couldn't hold out. Do you know what it is to desire a woman more than your own life?" he said, groping for somewhere to sit down. "Do you know what it's like?" he went on, flopping back in the armchair previously occupied by Don Podda. Without waiting for an answer he continued: "That is what happened to me. I have hungered for her enough to damn my soul, day in day out. I will tell you something I have not revealed even in Confession: I have sometimes hoped that Cosma would die. And when he did die I felt no more than a wonderful sense of relief. That's what I felt, God forgive me!" And he covered his face with his hands.

"Don't act that way! You have to tell me everything. For your own sake, for your peace of mind. That afternoon, then . . . "

"Of course, if you have someone who can corroborate this fact," ventured Sergeant Poli.

"Corroborate what?" stormed Donna Dolores.

"Corroborate the fact of your being at home that afternoon," explained Sergeant Poli. "If I were to ask your maid, for example?"

"She wouldn't be able to tell you," snapped Donna Dolores. "That Tuesday she had a nephew to look after."

"You have a good memory," commented Sergeant Poli.

"It will be hard to forget that afternoon," replied Donna Dolores.

And I should think so too. Sometimes I too come out with stupid things, believe me. They are often the most foolish things that slip out . . .

* * *

Bartolomeo bowed his head. "Yes, I went to Marreri, but I got there late. Too late. The thing had already happened. Cosma was dead. Dolores was there, not far from the body. We heard footsteps. It was Sisinnia running up, having heard the shots. Dolores was behaving like a madwoman, it was all I could do to drag her to a place of hiding. She was talking gibberish, saying that she had done it for both of us, for both of us, you understand? As if she'd driven me mad as well. She said that Cosma had threatened her, that he had found out the truth about Zenobi and the lambs, that he was beside himself with rage, that he loved Zenobi like a son. She even said he had threatened to send her back to where he had picked her up, practically out of the gutter. She said that if we didn't hurry up the Convento land would end up as part of Sisinnia's dowry. That was the way Cosma was made, Avvocato. He didn't see things as they are. For him it was all black or white, good or bad. I don't know exactly how it happened, I only know that she took the gun and shot him. What were we to do?"

"I cannot answer that, but I do know what you have to do now. There is an innocent person who is paying the price instead of you ... And at this very moment Donna Dolores is talking to Sergeant Poli ... "

* * *

My father spoke of that arrest as something beyond belief. He hadn't been so surprised even when they said that astronauts had landed and walked about on the moon. But in 1969 he was already ninety years old, God rest his soul. For him it was the world turned topsy-turvy: the rich in handcuffs and a penniless man set free.

Don Bartolomeo got twelve years imprisonment, and Donna Dolores was sentenced to thirty.

Sisinnia renounced her rights to the estate, and was

married in the clothes she was standing up in. Not a jot or a tittle did she carry home with her. When Zenobi and Sisinnia were married they begged Bustianu to be their witness, but he wouldn't hear of it. That they were as happy as possible was all he wished, and he wasn't needed. What mattered was to turn over a new leaf, start afresh, he said, and that what he had done was only his duty. What was all this business about making saints of the living? Out upon it, said he.

That was the way of Bustianu, who, however sociable he might appear to be, was always a man of solitude, ill at ease with the hustle and bustle. Nor did he like to give up his habits. Therefore, on the very afternoon of the wedding-breakfast, he was seen striding off towards Sant'Onofrio for his daily "ever belovèd".

Epilogue

AND NOW IT IS SUMMER AGAIN.

And here am I seated on the hilltop. From this height where I sit everything that meets the eye down there is douce and dolorous. Struck by the pitiless glare of summer. And behold me again, pierced to the heart by such a wealth of beauty, and stunned by it, all but overcome. The immensity of it is beyond words: immensity battering at frailty! A sublimity that catches you in the heart and the pit of the stomach. Space, space and still more space, spread out before my gaze. A space too overwhelming even for my own bulky body. In the sky-blue light of the valley, the sole divinity before whom it seems proper to bend the knee. If I were not a man I would weep at the sight of this. And sometimes I do so simply because I am a man. I take a deep breath and feel that all that blue light, that green, and the rolling stubblefields, make their secret way into my body and stream lines of poetry into my mind. Words like deep breaths and lips that tremble when my eyes light upon such colours. For this land is to me both my joy and my torment. It lures me to it yet thrusts me off. And I curse it, I curse it, even while I worship it. O cruel woman, embracing mother, insatiable lover!

Barren and dishevelled as may be, tossed down into the sea like a whore between the sheets! Afloat on the sea like a rudderless vessel. Soil like the sea, a crystal-clear emerald sea sparkling with gold. A land like the open sea which leads to who knows where, to who knows where? A sea that cradles it like a fondling mother. I am anchored to my rock-seat as on the fo'c'sle of a butting vessel tossed hither and thither amid the waves. I follow its motion like a madman hypnotized by the foaming surge that crashes up at every plunge of the keel, tempted to fling himself into that teeming void. O to be borne on by white iridescent nothingness, to flee this leaden bulk of mine and commit myself to the waves . . .

"For in that immensity my thought is drowned,
And a sweet thing it is to sink into this sea".